WINGS
OF
FIRE

WINGS OF FIRE

THE HIVE QUEEN

by
TUI T. SUTHERLAND

SCHOLASTIC INC.

This book was originally published in hardcover by Scholastic Press in 2019.

ISBN 978-93-9018-916-8

First edition: September 2020
This reprint edition : November 2023
Book design by Phil Falco
Printed in India at Saurabh Printers Pvt. Ltd.

For Wendy and Fiona, a pair of
kind and funny bookworms with dragon
hearts — Cricket and the bears and I
all think you are kindred spirits!

Tsetse Hive

Beetle Lake

Vinegaroon
Hive

Hornet Hive

Cicada Hive

Mantis
Hive

PANTALA

Tsetse Hive

Beet

A GUIDE TO THE
DRAGONS

Cicada Hive

Mantis Hive

Yellowjacket
Hive

Wasp
Hive

OF PANTALA

Bloodworm
Hive

HIVEWINGS

Description: red, yellow, and/or orange, but always mixed with some black scales; four wings

Abilities: vary from dragon to dragon; examples include deadly stingers that can extend from their wrists to stab their enemies; venom in their teeth or claws; a paralyzing toxin that can immobilize their prey; or boiling acid sprayed from a stinger on their tails

Queen: Queen Wasp

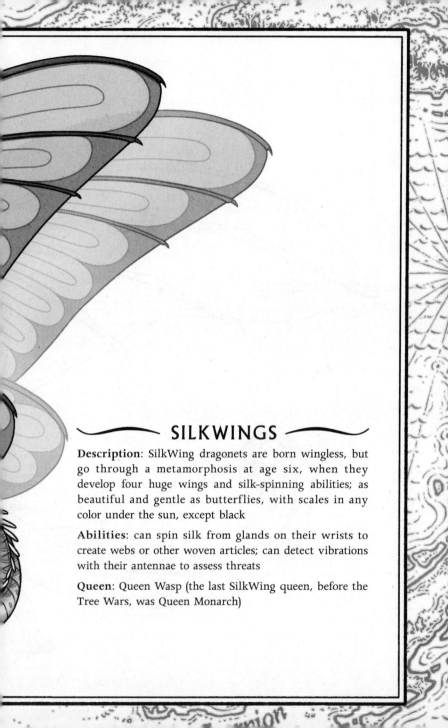

⎯ SILKWINGS ⎯

Description: SilkWing dragonets are born wingless, but go through a metamorphosis at age six, when they develop four huge wings and silk-spinning abilities; as beautiful and gentle as butterflies, with scales in any color under the sun, except black

Abilities: can spin silk from glands on their wrists to create webs or other woven articles; can detect vibrations with their antennae to assess threats

Queen: Queen Wasp (the last SilkWing queen, before the Tree Wars, was Queen Monarch)

LEAFWINGS

Description: wiped out during the Tree Wars with the HiveWings, but while they lived, this tribe had green and brown scales and wings shaped like leaves

Abilities: could absorb energy from sunlight and were accomplished gardeners; some were rumored to have unusual control over plants

Queen: last known queen of the LeafWings was Queen Sequoia, about fifty years ago, at the time of the Tree Wars

Tsetse Hive

Beetle Lake

Vinegaroon
Hive

Hornet Hive

Cicada Hive

Mantis
Hive

THE
LOST CONTINENT
PROPHECY

Turn your eyes, your wings, your fire
To the land across the sea
Where dragons are poisoned and dragons are dying
And no one can ever be free.

A secret lurks inside their eggs.
A secret hides within their book.
A secret buried far below
May save those brave enough to look.

Open your hearts, your minds, your wings
To the dragons who flee from the Hive.
Face a great evil with talons united
Or none of the tribes will survive.

The ocean swept across Moon's claws, as dark and speckled with stars as her own scales.

She'd always thought of the sea as the edge of the world. Once you got there, that was it; you couldn't go any farther.

But now she knew that wasn't true.

A dragon had been blown ashore, all the way from across the ocean — a dragon from a tribe nobody in Pyrrhia had ever seen before. A dragon with *four* wings instead of two; a dragon with long furling antennae and scales like sliced gems and the ability to spin silk that burned.

Luna was proof that there was a continent far on the other side of the sea, filled with strange dragons.

Dragons who need my help, she says.

Moon shivered. That couldn't be right. They didn't need *her*, of all dragons.

It was Moon's fault that Darkstalker had nearly taken over all of Pyrrhia; her fault that he'd killed so many IceWings, including their queen. She'd seen too much good in him and not enough of the bad. It was too soon for her to trust another dragon with a story of persecution. She wanted to use her visions to help the world . . . but she was not ready to have the fate of any more tribes in her talons.

But Luna wanted Moon to save all the SilkWings. Luna thought Moon was the second coming of Clearsight, who was apparently the number one beloved ancient goddess of Pantala.

So, no pressure there.

She can tell us what's going to happen next! Luna's brain sang. *She can see everything the HiveWings will do! She can predict Queen Wasp's next move and then the Chrysalis will know how to stop her!*

It was like that all day long. Luna had extremely grand ideas of Moon's abilities and shining dreams of how they would change everything.

She was so wound up, in fact, about Moon's ability to see the future that Moon hadn't quite found the courage yet to tell her she could also read minds.

It was really awkward, hearing all of Luna's thoughts about her and Qibli and Jerboa, and honestly it was getting more awkward every moment that Moon *didn't* tell her. If she'd had any extra skyfire, she would have slipped it to Luna somehow, to silence the pileup of expectations. But she didn't have any, so telling her wouldn't help much anyway.

I should, though. It's wrong not to.

Moon sighed.

She's seeing the future RIGHT NOW! came a thought, loud and clear, from right behind her. Moon winced and turned around to find Luna bounding over the sand. Well, trying to bound over the sand. The sand had a way of sinking out suddenly from under one's talons, so it was impossible to get any sort of bounding rhythm.

Those were partly Luna's thoughts. Moon sometimes got tangled up with them when they were too close to her own. She wasn't sure why, but there was something more entangling about Luna's mind than other dragons'.

"Why are you out here by yourself?" Luna asked, settling next to Moon in a spray of sand.

"I like to look at the moons sometimes," Moon answered, and then laughed. "That's my whole name, actually. Moonwatcher."

"My name means 'moon' in the old language, did you know that?" Luna asked. "Now it's a kind of moth." She dug a tiny hole in the sand in front of her and dropped a thread of flamesilk into it. The glow warmed Moon's talons.

"I didn't know that," Moon said, but she liked hearing it. It made her feel a little closer to Luna, who could be a bit intense sometimes. "What's the old language?"

Luna shrugged. "I don't know . . . the language everyone spoke in Pantala before Clearsight arrived?"

"Clearsight changed your language?" Moon said, surprised.

"I think so. I heard a story once, anyway, that we all speak Dragon because of her."

That explained why the Pantalans and Pyrrhians could understand each other, but Moon was still puzzled. Why didn't Clearsight learn *their* language instead?

Maybe she foresaw that we'd need to communicate with each other one day.

Or maybe she just hoped for it.

"Are you having a vision?" Luna asked hopefully.

"No!" Moon said. "Sorry . . . no, nothing yet."

Luna's wings slid down into the sand and she picked up a seashell, fiddling with it as though focusing on it would keep her from crying.

"I am really sorry, Luna," Moon said. "I don't know how to get you back to Pantala. Nothing in my visions has shown me that."

"I'm worried about my little brother," Luna said, throwing the seashell into the ocean. "And Swordtail. He must be losing his mind."

"Qibli will think of something," Moon said. "He usually does." She hesitated. "Luna . . . I don't know if it's a good idea to tell you this, but I've been hearing a prophecy in my head."

"A prophecy?" Luna echoed.

"It started with my vision of you in Jerboa's hut. I could hear a few words — and now, whenever I'm with you, it gets clearer and clearer. I don't completely understand it. And I'm afraid it might scare you."

"I'm not easily scared," Luna said. "Please tell me."

Moon sensed movement behind her, and then a few stray grumbling thoughts in a voice she recognized. Qibli had returned successful, then. Well, he could hear this, and so could the two dragons with him.

She took Luna's talons between her own, closed her eyes, and let her mind clear so the words of the prophecy could flow through her. She did not love this bit. Cryptic rhyming prophecies were not as useful as visions, in her opinion, and the last one had gone to a pretty terrifying place. But the last one had also saved her and her friends, so she couldn't ignore them.

"Turn your eyes, your wings, your fire," she whispered, *"to the land across the sea."* She felt Luna's shiver all through her own scales.

Where dragons are poisoned, and dragons are dying,
And no one can ever be free.
A secret lurks inside their eggs.
A secret hides within their book.
A secret buried far below
May save those brave enough to look.
Open your hearts, your minds, your wings
To the dragons who flee from the Hive.
Face a great evil with talons united
Or none of the tribes will survive."

Silence fell. Moon took a few deep breaths.

"I know the secret in the book," Luna said thoughtfully, "but what's the secret in the eggs? And the buried one . . . maybe that's the flamesilks. No one can ever be free, that's definitely true. A great evil. Hmm . . . maybe the HiveWings are the great evil?"

"Yeesh," Qibli said, coming up and nudging one of Moon's wings with his. "Didn't we *just* face a great evil? That should count, I say, if anyone asks me. Great evil, faced. Done. Take it off the to-do list."

She opened her eyes and smiled at him.

"Sounds like a new great evil," their friend Turtle said nervously from beside him. "Can I vote no on any more great evils in our lifetime?"

"Hey, Turtle," Moon said. "Hey, Tsunami."

The tall blue SeaWing founder of Jade Mountain Academy gave her an exasperated face. "Moon," she said. "I feel like I was *really clear* about not having anything to do with any more prophecies."

"They just happen to me," Moon protested. "I'm sorry!"

"Moon," Luna whispered, poking her surreptitiously with her tail. "Who are these dragons?"

"Oh — sorry, of course," Moon said. "Luna, this is our friend Turtle and his sister, Tsunami. They're from the SeaWing tribe. Thank you for going to get them, Qibli."

"Well, I *thought* that maybe *Turtle here* could *make us something*," Qibli said carefully, "which would perhaps *take us across the ocean*. So that Luna can get home."

"Oh?" Luna said, squinting at Turtle. "Like my silk sail?"

"But one we can steer — or something like that," Moon said. She and Qibli had agreed that they should wait to tell Luna about animus magic. If she got this excited and full of glorious vengeful plans over Moon's future-seeing, goodness knows how she would feel about real magic and all the things it could do to her enemy tribe.

Things we can't let her do, Qibli and Moon agreed. Animus magic was too dangerous.

But something made by animus magic that could get her home — that wouldn't hurt anyone. Qibli had offered to ask Turtle if he'd be willing to do that.

"Right," Turtle said. "Make something. So here's the thing. I can't."

"Oh," Moon said. "That's all right, Turtle, we understand. Your soul —"

"No, no," Turtle said, looking worried. "That's not it. I mean, I actually tried and . . . I can't."

Qibli made a face at Moon, like "It's true! I have no idea why!"

"Luna," Moon said. "Can you give us a moment?"

"Sure." The four-winged dragon turned and trudged slowly back to Jerboa's hut, limping on her injured ankle. *I knew I shouldn't have gotten my hopes up*, her mind thought sadly, and Moon felt awful for her.

"Poor lost dragon," Tsunami said. "It must be so

weird for her to be here, surrounded by strangers, with no way to get home."

"So what's wrong, Turtle?" Moon asked as soon as Luna was out of earshot.

"I don't know!" Turtle said, flinging up his wings. "I can't do *any* animus spells all of a sudden! I've tried all kinds of little things and nothing works!"

"Three moons," she said, blinking in confusion and alarm.

"Here's the really weird part — I don't think Anemone can, either," he said. "Right before Qibli came to get us, she was telling me about a spell she tried to restore Tamarin's sight. I'd been thinking of trying one for Starflight's, so we were comparing notes. But she said it didn't work, and she couldn't figure out why."

Turtle turned to give Qibli a severe look. "*I* suspect," he said, "that Qibli *broke* animus magic."

"ME?" Qibli cried. "What did I do?"

"The soul spells!" Turtle said. "Remember how you carefully planned them out with us? To protect our souls and make sure we can only do magic that doesn't affect another dragon's free will?"

"And no magic that's selfishly motivated," Qibli said. "Right. We all agreed safeguards would be helpful."

"Except I think it ruled out *everything*," Turtle said. "Maybe everything we do could be considered 'selfishly motivated' or affect *someone's* free will in some way. So now *none* of our spells work."

"Oh my goodness," said Moon.

"That is — no, that's — that's ridiculous," Qibli protested. "I did not *break* animus magic. I do not *think* I broke animus magic. That makes no — let me think about this."

"Did you try taking off your soul spell objects to see if it would work without them?" Moon asked.

"Anemone didn't want to," Turtle said, "but I did, just to try a small spell, and it still didn't work." He pointed at Qibli. "Broken."

"If it still didn't work without the soul spell, then it's *not the soul spell*," Qibli said. "And therefore *not me* who broke animus magic."

"It really feels like it is you, though," Turtle said.

"Maybe something else is going on," Moon said, worried. Darkstalker flashed through her mind, making plans, tinkering with dragons' powers. She knew he was gone now; he'd been turned into a dragonet with no powers and no memory of his past. But sometimes in her nightmares he still managed to mess with her friends. "What if someone else did this to you?" *Or left something behind that did this to you — some kind of safeguard. He could have done that, couldn't he? So if he ever lost his powers, so would everyone else?*

"There isn't anyone who could do that," Qibli said gently. He'd had to wake her up from some of those nightmares, so he knew what she was thinking as clearly as though he had mind-reading abilities, too. "This is just a glitch, not a sinister plan. We'll fix it."

"What about Jerboa?" Tsunami asked. "Is her magic working? She's an animus dragon, too, right?"

"Sort of. But she's an animus dragon who won't touch her magic," Moon said. "We can't ask her for help with this."

"Well, all right, then let's not," Tsunami said. "You guys, we don't need animus magic."

"We don't?" Turtle tipped his head up to look at her.

Tsunami grinned with all her teeth. "My friends and I solved plenty of problems without animus magic, thank you very much. It's called *being resourceful*. And *smart*. And *totally heroic, no prophecies required*."

"All right, Smarty McSquid," Turtle said. "So how would you and your resourceful, heroic friends solve this problem?"

"Well, step one is we need more information, right?" Tsunami said. "We want to go over there to see if Luna's stories are all true. To find out what's really going on and whether we should get involved."

"I think she's telling the truth, from what I can see in her mind," Moon said, "but it is hard to get a full picture of the situation. I wish we could go scout it out and see if there *is* a way we can help her."

"Maybe also what the great evil is?" Qibli suggested. "A heads-up about that would be super."

"So we need to get to the other continent," Tsunami said. "We don't need a magic flying sail thing to do that."

"Oh, ah," Qibli said. "Well, I mean. I did think of this. It's why I got you two, specifically. Just so we're clear that I thought of this first."

"Thought of what?" Turtle asked.

"To get to the lost continent, Turtle," Tsunami said, sweeping one wing out toward the ocean, "all you and I have to do is swim there."

PART ONE
THE GLITTERING HIVE

— CHAPTER 1 —

For most of her life, Cricket's best friends were books.

Books accepted you the way you were and shared all their secrets with you.

Books never told you to stop asking questions or accused you of being nosy and annoying. Books never said, "Cricket, you don't need to know that, mind your own business."

In books, everything had an explanation. She especially liked nonfiction: lots of facts and things had to make sense. If a question came up, eventually you got the answer. Every mystery was solved by the end. Facts fit together. When you wanted something explained, there it was, with no whispering or cold stares or slammed doors.

Another thing she liked about books was the fact that one of them had probably saved her life.

It was a giant book called *The Architecture of the Hives, Expanded Edition — now with sections on Hydroponics and Silk Bridges!*, which, technically, belonged to her mother, and therefore, technically, was off-limits to "tiny grubby dragonet talons," which was why two-year-old Cricket was hiding in a cupboard with it the first time everyone lost their minds.

"Why is this book so in *love* with itself?" little Cricket muttered. All she'd wanted to know was how to get from her home in Cicada Hive to the Temple of Clearsight in Wasp Hive, preferably in some clever, really fast way where she could be home that same night and nobody would notice she'd been gone. She just wanted to see it again, even if only for a moment.

But every sentence in this book was MILES too long and the author kept repeating himself over and over. Not to mention the never-ending rapturous paragraphs about every tiny curve and window and detail that "exemplified" Queen Wasp's "exquisite mental quality" and "eye for visual balance" or some such nonsense.

"This is not a book of answers," Cricket grumbled, flipping ahead. "This is a book of groveling." She paused on a full-page drawing of Wasp Hive. The book was nearly as big as she was, so the artist had lots of space to draw the temple at the heart of the hive. She rested her chin on her talons and stared dreamily at the perfect columns, the perfect dome on the roof, the perfect library and quiet pools all around the Temple of Clearsight.

She'd visited it for the first time only a few days earlier, when her sister, Katydid, took her as a treat for her second birthday. It was the most beautiful place Cricket had ever seen. Imagine being the Librarian and living there forever! Imagine being in charge of the Book of Clearsight, the most important book in the world — and being one of the only two dragons who *ever* got to read it.

Now *that* was a book with answers. Hundreds of years ago, Clearsight had written down her prophecies of every important thing that would happen after her death, starting in her time and reaching far into the future. If Cricket read it, she'd really know everything! Maybe her brain would finally stop buzzing with questions all the time. Maybe she'd finally feel like everything made sense.

Cricket wanted the world to feel more like a book: Here is a question, so here is an answer. Here are the mysteries of the universe; now here is everything you want to know about them.

If her life were a book, she could check the index and go straight to the page that would tell her why her parents were always fighting or why her mother didn't love her. She would read the chapter about how Katydid was always sad, and then she could read about how to fix it to make her sister happy.

Those were the big mysteries of two-year-old Cricket's life. She had no idea that there was an even bigger one hiding below the surface of her entire tribe, or that she might be the key to solving it.

A shriek from outside tore through the hum of Cricket's thoughts, startling her so much she banged her head on the top of the cupboard and nearly knocked over the little flame-silk lamp she'd smuggled in. She caught it with a flare of panic and relief. If she set her mother's book on fire, she might as well go ahead and burn the whole house down to hide the evidence — she'd be in just as much trouble either way.

The scream came again, and Cricket nearly leaped out of the cabinet to investigate. But before she could, heavy talons entered the kitchen, and she covered the lamp quickly with her wings.

"There is a traitor in this Hive," said her mother's voice, but not her mother's voice at all. **"Do not let him escape."**

Cricket held her breath, more terrified than she even understood. Who was her mother talking to? Why did she sound all . . . wrong?

More talonsteps entered the room — this had to be Katydid, the only other dragon at home — but without any further conversation, the two of them ran out the front door.

Cricket pushed the cupboard door open a crack and peeked out. The kitchen was deserted, although she could hear a lot of commotion on the street outside.

Curiosity and fear went to war within her, and as often happened in Cricket's life, curiosity won. She left the book hidden, took the lamp with her, and slipped out of the cabinet, hurrying upstairs to her mother's office, which had a window with a view of the street.

It was the same street she flew down every day: houses built of treestuff, turquoise mosaic tiles glittering in the light of the flamesilk lamps, neatly tended gardens here and there, a line of black stones inlaid in the ground to show young dragonets the way to school.

But instead of her polite, peaceful neighbors and the usual strolling dragons, the street was now bristling with marching rows of teeth and claws. Cricket had never heard the word *mob*, but when she did, years later, she thought it was almost right for what she'd seen — but not quite. The dragons below her weren't enraged or in chaos. They moved in eerie unison and near-complete silence as they surrounded the one dragon who was out of sync with the rest, cutting off all his possible escape routes.

He cowered in the center of the glaring circle, his red-and-black-striped wings folded in tightly. He looked quite old, older than most dragons Cricket knew. Maybe sixty or a hundred? She didn't really know how to guess the ages of grown-up dragons. But he was quite big and his scales were a little dull and he moved in a tired, aching-bones kind of way.

"Please just let me go!" he shouted at the crowd. His eyes flickered white for a moment and then dark again. "I promise I'm not a threat to you! I don't want to be like them!"

"That is not an option," the surrounding dragons said in one voice.

It wasn't just the voice that was wrong. Their eyes . . . their eyes were all wrong, too.

Cricket felt a spasm of fear. Throughout the crowd, the dragons' eyes were all white, like pure glassy marbles, like empty snakeskins, like dead blood-sucked grubs.

Three of them stepped forward with their claws or tails raised to point menacing stingers at their prey. Their faces were blank, cold, and merciless. They looked ready to kill without a flicker of emotion.

And one of them was Katydid.

Cricket ducked below the window frame, her heart beating frantically.

What is happening? What is wrong with my sister?

What's wrong with all *of them?*

She heard another scream from below and forced herself to peek out again.

The old dragon was being marched away down the street, struggling weakly, surrounded by a phalanx of dragons who were almost all Cricket's friends and neighbors. Except now they had been transformed into something else, something dark and no longer dragon, and Cricket wasn't sure she'd ever be able to look at them the same way again.

Her eyes caught on a flutter of blue near a doorway, and she realized that a SilkWing was there, pressing herself back into the shadows to stay out of the way. The SilkWing's eyes were normal, but her expression was fearful and puzzled.

Cricket's gaze flicked across the houses quickly and she spotted five more SilkWings watching from doorways and windows. None of them had the snakeskin eyes. A couple wore resigned expressions, as though they'd seen this before, but at least all of them had *some* emotion on their faces. None of them were empty, like the HiveWings down below.

So whatever's happening, it's only happening to HiveWings. It's not affecting the SilkWings . . .

. . . or me.

Her mind leaped onto this puzzle, preferring it enormously to the other option of contemplating the horror of what she'd just seen.

Is it because I'm too young? But that couldn't be it — there were little dragonets everywhere in the crowd, intoning the same words as the other HiveWings. Bombardier, the most annoying dragonet in her class, was among the ones who'd marched the old dragon away. Even Midge, the tiniest dragonet on the block, who had hatched a month ago, was down there with her eyes blank and teeth bared.

Maybe this was something parents taught their kids to do, but because Cricket's parents didn't like her, they'd forgotten (or neglected) to do it.

Maybe the other HiveWings had learned it in school, sometime when Cricket was reading under her desk and not paying attention.

Maybe there were secret meetings for all the other HiveWings except her, and she wasn't invited because she asked too many questions.

But Katydid . . .

Katydid would have told her if all the HiveWings did something together that Cricket should know about. She would have taught her how to blank out her eyes and march with the others and threaten old dragons and look totally scary.

More important, Katydid would never actually do any of those things.

Except she did. I just saw her.

A door slammed downstairs. Cricket glanced outside and saw the HiveWings dispersing. The ones who had marched the old dragon away were still visible in the distance, but everyone else was blinking and yawning and heading back indoors.

Uh-oh. If Katydid was one of the ones marching off . . . that meant the dragon who'd just come into the house would be Mother.

Cricket ran out of her mother's office and dove into the nearest closet just in time. Through the crack in the door, she saw her mother stomp past the closet and into her office in a blur of orange and black scales, her wings buzzing slightly the way they did when she was annoyed (usually at Cricket).

Come to think of it, it was really strange for Cricket's mother to leave her office during her morning work hours. Cricket and Katydid weren't allowed to make even the slightest noise before noon in case they disturbed her.

The office door slid shut and Cricket let out the breath she'd been holding. A part of her desperately wanted to burst in and ask her mother all the questions swarming in her head. Starting with, Would Katydid come back? How soon? And, of course, things like, So WHAT IN THE HIVE WAS THAT?

But some deeper instinct protected her. This once, she didn't let her curiosity win.

Instead she crept up to Katydid's room on the top floor and curled herself under her sister's dark blue silk blankets. She closed her eyes and tried not to cry and waited.

It was late that night when Katydid finally returned, exhausted and windblown. Cricket's father had come home earlier and Cricket had listened to both her parents eating dinner and hissing at each other. Neither one had looked for her or called to ask her to join them. But that was normal.

Katydid was the only one in the house who tried to organize family meals. She was the one who made sure Cricket was fed and got to school on time. In a year, she'd be the one who finally took Cricket to an eye doctor to get her glasses.

She was the only dragon Cricket loved.

Her heart lit up as Katydid came through the door. Cricket bounded out of the blankets, grabbed her sister's shoulders, and stared into her face. Her eyes were back to normal.

"Ow, gentle," Katydid scolded, but kindly. She removed Cricket's claws and rolled her shoulders as though they were sore. "I had to fly to Wasp Hive and back today, so take it easy on me."

"Why?" Cricket demanded. "Why did you have to? What did you do to that old dragon? What happened to your eyes this morning? Why was everyone acting so awful and weird?" All the questions she'd been bottling up all day spilled out of her, along with the tears she thought she'd beaten. "What was that voice? Why did you look so mean? Katydid, what happened to you?"

Katydid was supposed to say something reassuring. She was supposed to shrug and laugh and explain how it was a HiveWing game and Cricket would learn it next week, not to worry, nothing important.

But instead Katydid stared at her, with the least reassuring expression possible on her face.

"What happened to me . . ." she said. "Didn't it happen to you, too?"

"No!" Cricket cried. "I mean, I don't know what it was, but I sure didn't get all super possessed and freaky-looking and mean like everyone else I could see. Your eyes were totally white, Katydid! And you were growling at that old dragon! Couldn't you see how scared he was?"

"But that was a whole-Hive command," Katydid said. "All talons out. Every dragon in the Hive was included. There's no *way* you could have been left out." Her kind orange-yellow face was all worry. Cricket had never seen her sister look so anxious.

"Left out of what?" Cricket asked nervously.

Katydid rubbed her forehead and sidled over to close the door, although their parents were probably both asleep already and usually never came up to the sisters' rooms anyway.

"It doesn't happen often," she said softly, "but sometimes Queen Wasp . . . controls dragons. I mean, not just with orders and soldiers. I mean she gets into your brain and makes you do, um . . . anything she wants you to."

"What?" Cricket said. "How? That's — *what*?"

"It's very efficient," Katydid pointed out. "Like today, when there was a traitor who'd run away from her and was trying to hide out in our Hive. Queen Wasp can take over all the dragons in the Hive at once and find him immediately. Then we catch him, and she releases most everybody while a few of us escort him back to her."

"But — do you want to?" Cricket asked. "Can she do it anytime she wants, from anywhere? What if you're busy? Or what if you don't want to do what she says?"

Her sister shook her head. "You *do* want to," she said. "She *is* the queen, Cricket. If she were standing next to you giving an order, you'd do it no matter what, of course. This is basically the same, except she doesn't have to be everywhere at once."

It's not *the same at* all, Cricket thought rebelliously. "So your talons move and your voice speaks and your wings fly and there's nothing you can do to stop it?" she asked. "You can't even say, no thank you, not today?"

Katydid threw out her wings. "Of course not! Cricket, you wouldn't really ever say that to the queen, surely. Be serious."

If she ordered me to stab someone, I would, Cricket thought. *If she asked me to drag away an elderly dragon who was crying, I* would *say no.*

She thought. She hoped.

She wasn't sure. There was a difference between being brave in a book and brave in real life, so there certainly might be a difference between the Cricket in her head and a real Cricket standing in front of the actual terrifying queen.

"But how does it work?" Cricket asked. "I've never seen anything like that in any science book."

"I have no idea," Katydid said tiredly, which was how a lot of conversations between the sisters ended. Cricket wasn't ready to let this one go yet, though.

"And why doesn't it work on me?" she pressed. "Is Mother right that there's something wrong with me?"

"No!" Katydid protested. "Of course not. I don't know why. But why doesn't matter — what matters is how to protect you so no one realizes it doesn't work on you. You'll have to stay alert for when it happens. We'll find places for you to hide. The good news is she doesn't do it very often. I'll keep you safe, Cricket, I promise."

"You think I'll be in trouble if Queen Wasp finds out?" Cricket said in a small voice.

"I'm afraid maybe," Katydid admitted. She put her wings around Cricket and they leaned into each other.

"But — if she takes over your brain — won't she know about me, now that you know?" Cricket asked.

"No, it doesn't work like that," Katydid said. "She doesn't get into our thoughts and secrets and everything we know. She just controls what our bodies are doing for a little while."

Cricket shuddered. That sounded *completely horrible*, plus also it was extremely weird and unsettling that Katydid didn't *think* it sounded completely horrible.

But Katydid kept her promise. For the next four years, Katydid covered for her, and Cricket learned to be careful and how to hide quickly until the commands passed. The question of "why" *did* matter to her, and she did all the research she could, but with no luck. Still, she kept the secret and she was clever and safe and as cautious as an impulsive, curious little dragonet could be.

Until the most beautiful dragon Cricket had ever seen fell over a wall into her school courtyard, and all her caution threw itself out the window.

She couldn't exactly say why she'd helped Blue hide — or why she'd told him her secret — or why she'd left the safety of her Hive to fly across the savanna with him on a hazardous rescue mission. Maybe those were all answers she'd find at the end of her own book.

For now, all she had were consequences. She was a fugitive, wanted for stealing the Book of Clearsight and helping flamesilks escape the queen. The Book of Clearsight had *not* contained all the answers to the universe, after all. Worse, Cricket's secret Hive-mind immunity had been exposed in the Temple, and now the queen knew that she was different — that the mind control didn't work on her. Cricket would never be able to go home again.

But on the other talon, now she had Blue in her life. And as she sat by his softly glowing cocoon in an underground cave deep below Pantala, she decided she had no regrets about what she'd done . . . except maybe one.

She really

really

REALLY wished she'd brought a book with her.

Cricket sighed and stretched out her wings. Four more DAYS of sitting in a cave with nothing to read? She was seriously going to lose her mind.

It had been very dramatic and romantic when Blue's golden flamesilk had begun spiraling from his wrists and they'd come running down into this secret cave and she'd knelt beside him and pledged to be there when he woke up and to stay beside him always . . .

But now he was peacefully snoozing away, growing his wings, and she was SO BORED.

She stood up and circled his cocoon. It was a beautiful silvery-gold color, but she missed the blue and purple of Blue's scales. She wished she could see even a hint of them through the silk. She knew that when she did, that would be a sign he was almost ready to come out.

She hoped his friends would be back by then. She hoped Luna and Swordtail and Sundew were safe. How long had she been down here? Her sense of time seemed muffled by the caves, but she thought a whole day might have passed. Had Luna been blown out to sea, or recaptured by the HiveWings? Had Swordtail followed her? Was Sundew all right?

It felt a little odd to worry about Sundew, who had been her captor only a few days earlier. Sundew — well, really Sundew's parents — had forced Cricket to help steal the Book of Clearsight, which led to this whole mess. But then Sundew had helped her rescue Blue and Luna, so that more than balanced the scales, in Cricket's opinion.

And the truth was, she kind of liked the fierce LeafWing. Sundew let herself be mad and always said what she really thought and made all her own decisions, even when her parents didn't like it, and Cricket didn't know any HiveWings like that. Prickly opinions that stuck out in the Hives tended to get smashed down fairly quickly.

Are all LeafWings like that? Brave enough to do their own thing, no matter what anyone else thinks?

Sundew's parents, Belladonna and Hemlock, would have preferred to keep Cricket and Swordtail under their wings until they found another use for them. It was Sundew who had insisted on helping them free the flamesilks instead.

And she'd kept the Book of Clearsight, instead of giving it to them. Cricket's parents would NEVER have agreed to that or trusted her with something so important. Belladonna and Hemlock had grumbled, but when Sundew put her talons down, they accepted it.

She didn't have to help fight the HiveWings who spotted Luna and Swordtail, either, Cricket thought. *But she didn't even hesitate.*

Cricket wished she could ever be that sure of herself. Sundew moved like a dragon who'd already found all the answers to her questions.

It was really quiet in the caves this far under the earth. If she sat still and concentrated, she could hear water trickling in the distance. And every once in a while, she heard weird little squeaky echoes, which she suspected — all right, she *hoped* — were more of those little reading monkeys, like the one she and Blue had seen at the bottom of a sinkhole on the savanna.

If I could find them, maybe I could borrow one of THEIR books, she thought wistfully. Which made her laugh at herself. Of course she wouldn't be able to understand the little reading monkey language (if that's what it was). Plus her claws would be too big for their tiny books.

But imagine holding a book by *another species* in her talons! What if she could translate it? What would it say? What did monkeys think about? What were their stories about? What did they know that dragons didn't? It felt as if her head might explode, thinking about everything she might discover. *In another life, where studying them could have been my destiny.*

A noise sounded from the stone passages beyond the cave.

Cricket froze, all senses on alert.

It came again . . . the scratch of claws on rock. The sound of a tail slithering along the floor.

Someone else was in the caves.

CHAPTER 2

Cricket held her breath, her mind frantically darting through her options. Could she pretend she was guarding the cocoon? That maybe Queen Wasp had given her a secret mission?

Not if the dragon who was coming had white eyes. If Queen Wasp was inside this dragon's brain, she'd recognize Cricket as the dragon who'd stolen the Book of Clearsight and two of her flamesilks. She'd be able to raise the entire continent to descend on this cave in a heartbeat. And there was no way Cricket could hide Blue before they arrived.

She stepped in front of his cocoon anyway and tried to make her face look menacing.

But the dragon who appeared in the doorway was the green and gold of summer leaves, with two wings instead of four. Cricket had never been so relieved to see a scowl that fierce.

"Sundew!" she cried, leaping toward her. "You're all right!"

"No thanks to any of you," Sundew grumbled. She winced as she stepped into the cave, and Cricket spotted a trickle of blood running down her shoulder.

"What happened?" Cricket asked, catching Sundew's pouches as the LeafWing threw them off and setting them against the wall. "Have you seen Swordtail and Luna? I'm so sorry I couldn't fly up and help you — not that I'm much use in a fight anyway — but Blue's Metamorphosis started and I had to get him somewhere safe." She waved her wings at the glowing lump behind her. "What did you do to the HiveWings? Do they know where we are?"

She felt the shape of the Book of Clearsight in the last pouch and laid it carefully, reverently, on the stone floor. The queen had lied to everyone about the Book, but it was still very old and pretty sacred and most important a BOOK (Something to read! At last!).

"I led them away," Sundew said, shaking raindrops off her wings. "I flew south. Those smug moss-brained monsters chased me all the way to Lake Scorpion, and then I lost them and came back the very annoyingly long way around Dragonfly Bay. It's pouring outside — easy to lose a dragon in a storm." She shook her head. "Didn't see Luna anywhere, but I did find this bedraggled unhelpful mess." Sundew ducked out into the passageway and Cricket followed her.

Swordtail lay sprawled on the cave floor, unconscious. He

seemed much wetter than Sundew, as though she had just dredged him up from the bottom of the ocean. Long strands of seaweed were tangled through his horns and his talons and wrapped around his dark blue wings.

"By the Book, where has he been?" Cricket asked, crouching beside him to study his face. "Is he all right?"

Sundew shrugged disinterestedly. "He's alive. I found him like this on a rock in the bay. He's lucky I found him instead of a HiveWing, although I was pretty tempted to leave him there." She grabbed one of his back talons and started dragging him into Blue's cave. Cricket followed, trying to hold Swordtail's head above the bumpy rocks.

"But he was alone?" she asked as Sundew dropped the SilkWing in a heap beside the flamesilk cocoon.

"My guess is Luna got blown out to sea and he tried to follow her," Sundew said. She stretched her wings again and shook out her talons as though her shoulder hurt. "But the storm chucked him into a boulder instead. Which he deserved, if you ask me. Did you see him fly off and leave me fighting two HiveWings alone? I mean, sure, Luna is great and I know he just got her back and all and I get it; I have a one true love, too."

"You DO?" Cricket said, fascinated. "Who?"

"But on the other talon, HiveWings!" Sundew went on, ignoring her. "With pointy stabby bits! Plus, he left you guys in danger, too, which he apparently didn't even think about."

"He probably thinks you could take on nine times that many HiveWings by yourself and be all right," Cricket admitted. "I mean, that's what *I* think." She was still wrapping her mind around the last revelation. *Sundew has a one true love! Another LeafWing, I guess. What kind of dragon would Sundew fall in love with? Is it someone equally terrifying?*

"Hm," Sundew said, looking a little mollified. "Well, that would be the first sign of life from his brain, that's for sure."

"I guess he never found Luna. And you didn't see where she went?" Cricket glanced worriedly at Blue's cocoon. Could he hear anything through the layers of silk? Probably not; she was pretty sure Metamorphosis was kind of a long dreamless sleep. But how would he react when he came out and discovered that the sister he'd worked so hard to rescue was . . . gone?

"No, but I got a survivor vibe from her. That one can take care of herself, I think." Sundew picked up one of Swordtail's wings and dropped it with a wet thwapping sound. "Moon-faced, self-aggrandizing opinions to the contrary."

"But wait . . . how did you get him back here?" Cricket asked wonderingly. Sundew was about the same size as Swordtail, maybe a little smaller. There was no way the

LeafWing could have carried him across the bay and into the cave, especially in the storm, and especially if she was trying not to be noticed.

"Has anyone ever told you that you ask a lot of questions?" Sundew snapped.

"Oh, yes," Cricket said. "All the time."

Sundew crinkled her nose, which Cricket hoped was her "trying not to laugh" expression. "Well, *stop* for a few heartbeats while I catch my breath."

"All right," Cricket said, although wanting to know so many things and not being able to find them out felt like small creatures buzzing under her scales. "Can I get you some water for that?" She pointed to Sundew's injury. "If you stay with Blue, I can go find the underground river. It can't be far if we can hear it so well from here." Maybe she'd have a better chance of getting answers if she did something helpful first.

"Yes, all right," Sundew said. "At least it'll be quiet while you're gone." She pointed to one of her pouches. "There's a moss in there that can absorb nearly a whole pond. Take some of that with you."

Cricket dug out a talonful of moss and bounded off into the caves. It wasn't hard to make a mental map in her head as she followed the sound of water through the tunnels.

The river she found was more of a stream, although she guessed it would get stronger if she kept walking down it, toward the sound of rapids. But a little bit of water was all she needed, so she dipped the clump of moss in until it was well soaked, then headed back to Blue's cave.

Sundew muttered, "Thank you" as she took the moss and pressed it to the cut on her shoulder. Cricket hovered for a moment, wondering if she could help more, but the green dragon looked extra scowly and prone to biting, so Cricket decided it would be safer to back away for a little while.

"I hope Luna's all right," she said, circling Swordtail. "I wonder if she can swim." At least Swordtail was unconscious and therefore unlikely to snap at her. Cricket started untangling the seaweed from his wings, piling it up nearby. There was a *lot* of it. Was it edible? She hadn't eaten in . . . hmmm. She wasn't sure, but it seemed like a very long time. She'd probably have to starve for another day or two before she'd find gloppy wet seaweed at all appetizing, though.

"How long ago did you find him?" she asked. The pile of seaweed oozed and squished as she added more to it. *Squelp. Thwerk. Splaf.* "Do you think he'll wake up soon? I wonder if he'll stay to watch Blue come out or go off looking for Luna again. Maybe she's stranded on another island in the bay. So maybe she'll come back and find us? Should we leave a message in the beach cave so she'll come down here? But no, then Queen Wasp's scouts might see it — we sure don't want them finding us. Hey, how did you find me?"

"AARRRRGH," Sundew growled. "You don't even KNOW that you're doing it. Here, wake him up so you can bother someone else." She grabbed one of her pouches and threw it to Cricket.

"Oh, sorry! Sorry," Cricket said. She had in fact forgotten about not asking Sundew any more questions during her trip back and forth to the river. "What's in here? I mean — um, I'll figure it out!" She flipped open the pouch, which was woven out of large, shiny, waterproof leaves, and found three neat compartments with different bundles in each. She hoped none of them contained alarming insects like the ones she'd seen Sundew fight dragons with.

"Middle section," Sundew said. "Crush one under his nose." She threw a few berries in her mouth and lay down with her back to Cricket, Swordtail, and Blue.

Inside the middle compartment of the pouch, wrapped in a soft covering of cobwebs, Cricket found a trio of weird-looking plants. Each was shiny red, mottled with yellow streaks and curved in around itself so there was a hollow in the middle and a point at one end. Cricket carefully took one out, held it under Swordtail's snout, and squished it between her claws.

The scent that came out was unexpectedly horrible, and strong enough to make her own eyes water. Swordtail grunted, his face twitching in distress. Cricket held the plant in place as long as she could, then ran across the cave to throw it out into the passageway.

When she came back, Swordtail was blinking and trying to sit up, rubbing his eyes. He unraveled a long strand of seaweed from his legs and managed to roll upright. His bewildered gaze took in the flamesilk cocoon and then Cricket.

Cricket wanted to help, but the truth was, Swordtail made her a little nervous. She knew he was Blue's best friend and Blue trusted him, but he was kind of loud and mad and she got the feeling he didn't like her very much.

There had always been dragons in her classes who didn't like her because she got the right answer or made the class run long with her questions, or because she'd rather be reading a book than playing one of their recess games. Or because she understood equations better than she understood other dragons, and sometimes she was just awkward and out of step with everyone else and, you know what, normal conversations were hard; didn't anyone else find them hard?

But Swordtail disliked her entirely because she was a HiveWing. She couldn't argue with that. She couldn't help being a HiveWing, and she couldn't defend anything her tribe had done, and it wasn't useful to keep saying "but I'm not like them!" over and over. She just had to hope that eventually she'd do enough to prove she could be trusted.

Cricket glanced over at the resting LeafWing, wishing she could talk to her instead. Sundew hated HiveWings even more than Swordtail did, but she seemed OK with Cricket, in her own ferocious way. Cricket suspected there was someone almost as kind as Blue under all Sundew's layers of thorns, although so far she'd only caught glimpses of her.

The LeafWing was also really smart and knew a million things about plants and insects that Cricket had never learned in school. Cricket kind of wished she could open up Sundew's brain and read it like a book — especially all the parts about LeafWings and where they'd gone and how they'd survived. Sundew wouldn't answer *any* of those questions, except with growling.

"Where's Luna?" Swordtail asked right away, raking another talonful of seaweed off his neck.

"I don't know," Cricket said. "I saw her silk get caught in the wind and carry her out to sea, but Blue's Metamorphosis was starting, so I had to bring him down here. I don't know what happened next. What did you see? What happened to you?"

Swordtail rubbed his forehead as if it hurt. "I tried to follow her — but the storm —" He took a step toward the corridor and stumbled over a trailing piece of seaweed. "I have to go find her."

"Shouldn't you rest for a bit first?" Cricket suggested. "Sundew says it's pouring outside. And you were just unconscious —"

"I'll be fine," he insisted. "Luna needs me." He took another staggering step toward the door.

"Don't be a skunk cabbage," Sundew said grumpily, turning her head to frown at him. "You're entirely useless to any dragon in the state you're in."

"But —" He paused, struggling for words, and then slumped, perhaps feeling the extent of the battering the storm had given him.

"Look for her tomorrow," Cricket suggested. "Or as soon as you're dry, or after you sleep, or whatever you want. But you'll be much more likely to find her with well-rested wings and a clear head, don't you think? Maybe we can do some calculations about wind speed and currents and figure out where she might be. It would help if I had some books, though; I've never studied the ocean on this side of the continent. I wonder how buoyant flamesilk is. Do you know anything about it?"

Swordtail sighed, although Cricket couldn't tell if it was an exasperated sigh or a resigned sigh or just exhaustion. "Not much," he said. He turned away from the door, limped over to Blue's cocoon, and touched it lightly with his talons. "Poor Blue. Was he . . . did he seem scared?"

"Maybe a little," Cricket said, "but he was very brave. He was mostly worried about you and Luna."

Swordtail rubbed at his eyes. "That sucks. I wish we'd been here for him."

She guessed they were both thinking the same thing — that they hoped Luna would be here when Blue woke up.

The glow of Blue's cocoon lit Swordtail's face as he leaned down to study the silken strands. "So I guess this means Blue's a flamesilk, too?" he said.

"It looks like it," Cricket agreed.

"Good," said Sundew.

They both turned and blinked at her.

"Good? Why? What does that mean?" Cricket asked.

"It's useful," Sundew answered. "Our cause doesn't need another normal boring timid SilkWing. But a flamesilk — that's fantastic."

"You think Blue is going to be useful . . . for the *LeafWings*?" Swordtail said in a dangerous voice.

"How?" Cricket took an instinctive step closer to the cocoon, as though Blue might sense her protection through the silk. "What do you think he could do?"

Sundew flicked her wings back and tipped her head. "A few hundred awesome fiery things," she said. "Starting with the most obvious: he's going to burn down all the Hives for us."

—— CHAPTER 3 ——

"No way!" Cricket cried. "Blue would never do that!"

"Burn down *all the Hives*," Swordtail echoed, sounding a little more awestruck than Cricket was comfortable with.

"Is that really your plan?" Cricket asked Sundew. She knew the LeafWings were here for a reason, and she thought she understood how angry they were at the HiveWings — but this was so much more violent than she'd expected. Did the LeafWings want to restart the war? Even after they lost so badly the last time? "I thought you said you just wanted the Book!"

Sundew stabbed at the pouch with the Book of Clearsight in it. "Yes, when we thought the stupid thing would tell us the future. Instead it's completely useless. So what else are we supposed to do?"

"*Not* burn down the Hives?!" Cricket suggested.

"They're so big," Swordtail murmured. He gazed up at the ceiling, as though he was imagining an entire city on fire. "Even Luna never suggested destroying a whole *Hive*."

"You'd be starting the Tree Wars all over again," Cricket said. "If you try to burn any of the Hives, Queen Wasp will send her whole army after you."

"She's not the only one with an army," Sundew said, scowling. "This time we'll be ready. The new Tree Wars will go very differently — especially if we start with burning the HiveWings out of their cities."

Are there that many LeafWings left? Cricket wondered. *A whole army of them?*

"Blue won't help you burn cities," Cricket said to Sundew. She was sure of that. "He would never do anything to hurt anyone."

Swordtail gave her a strange look. "Excuse me," he said, "but you barely know Blue. *I'm* the one who's been his best friend basically his whole life."

"Well then, do *you* see him burning down Hives all across Pantala?" Cricket asked.

"Maybe if he had a good enough reason," Swordtail muttered.

"Exactly." Sundew nodded, as though she believed any dragon could be turned into a murderer with the right motivation.

Cricket didn't believe that. At least, she couldn't believe it of Blue. She'd spent almost her whole life watching her friends and family turn into cold-eyed tools for the queen, doing things they'd never do if they had the choice. Blue was the absolute opposite of all that. He had free will. And with it, he always chose to be kind, to do the right thing.

Didn't he?

In the five days you've known him? a voice like Swordtail's whispered in her head. *You think you know this dragon now? Because you hid together, freed Swordtail, broke into the Temple, and stole the Book? Does he always do the right thing, or could it be that you just think that "the right thing" is whatever he chooses to do?*

What if he thinks burning down Hives is "the right thing" to do to save his tribe?

"Is that why you came back here instead of going to your parents?" she asked Sundew, trying to shake off her doubts. "You came for Blue?"

"Yes." Sundew shrugged. "I'd rather have Luna. She got so excellently mad about the Book of Clearsight that I'm sure she'd help us. I'd take her with me to burn the world down any day. But if we don't have Luna, we need Blue."

"We'll have Luna!" Swordtail blurted. "She's coming back! I'll find her!" He paced agitatedly from the cocoon to the door and back again. Sundew crinkled her nose and drew her tail out of the splatter zone from the seaweed still dangling off him.

"Blue will help you, but not by hurting other dragons," Cricket said stubbornly. "How would burning down all the Hives help the LeafWings anyway?"

"Also, there's a problem: even if Blue or Luna agreed to help you," Swordtail chimed in, "one flamesilk can't burn down a whole Hive. Let alone all nine of them."

"Well, he can try," Sundew said. "Or we start with Wasp Hive and then use those buried flamesilks to help with the rest. We have to do *something*. Whatever takes out as many HiveWings as we can."

"Sundew!" Cricket cried. "How can you *say* that? That's my tribe! I know some of them are terrible, but you don't really want to kill *all* of them, do you?"

Now Sundew was scowling so ferociously that Cricket could almost see sparks coming out of her wings. Her claws dug into the stone below her. "Why not? That's *exactly* what they tried to do to us!"

"I know, but doesn't that make you see how wrong it is?" Cricket said.

"No," Sundew growled. "*We* didn't do anything to them. They *deserve* it. They deserve to be wiped out. Every single HiveWing." She frowned and dropped her gaze to the pouch with the Book of Clearsight in it. "Except you, but you're different."

"What if I'm not the only one who's different? Or what about the littlest dragonets?" Cricket said desperately. "It's been so long since the Tree Wars. So many HiveWings weren't even alive back then. Or what about the ones who refused to fight? There were protesters, I know there were; I read about them. There were HiveWings who tried to say no to Queen Wasp. There were some who wanted to help the LeafWings and save the trees. What about them?"

She stopped suddenly, struck by a thought that she couldn't believe she'd never had before.

How could there have been protesters?

Wouldn't Queen Wasp have shut them down with her mind control? She wouldn't have allowed dissent during her war; she would never have let anyone disagree with her. So . . . how did they?

Were they like me? Why couldn't she control them?

"Protesters," Sundew scoffed. "Shouting enthusiastic rhymes at the sky while their friends slaughtered us. Maybe that would have been useful if they'd kept it up, but they all vanished by the end. Not a single HiveWing objected when the last tree was cut down."

"Maybe they couldn't." Cricket's mind was racing now. "Maybe the queen had them all in her power by then." Did she get rid of any dragons who couldn't be controlled? Or . . . was it possible Wasp hadn't been born with her mind-control powers? Had they come to her sometime during the war?

"Personally, I vote yes for burning down the Hives," Swordtail offered suddenly. "I think Luna will be all for it, if we can't convince Blue."

Cricket whirled toward him. "Haven't you thought about this at all? Imagine a Hive burning. Who dies first?" She pushed her glasses up, wishing she didn't sound so nervous and shaky. "SilkWing dragonets, Swordtail! They're the ones who won't be able to fly to safety! Innocent, wingless dragonets in their eggs and cocoons and schools and parks. And in your webs! The webs are connected to the Hives; if the cities burn, so do your homes! Most of the HiveWings will escape and be fine, but how would you save all the little SilkWings?"

Swordtail stared down at his claws, looking pale.

"Killing off all the HiveWings — or trying to — won't solve anything," Cricket said to Sundew. "It'll just start another war that'll be even bloodier than the last, and this time Queen Wasp will hunt you to the very ends of the continent to make sure you're gone. And maybe all the SilkWings, too, if she thinks some of you were in on it."

"She won't kill us," Swordtail said bitterly. "She needs our silk and our fire. We're valuable resources."

"She can make your lives worse, though," Cricket pointed out.

Swordtail seized a talonful of seaweed and threw it against the wall with a damp *splat*. He stomped on her neat pile again and again, flattening it into a dark morass like crushed eels and bleeding squids.

"I just want to *hurt* them," he said. "I want them to feel what it's like to be powerless. I want *them* to be stabbed with nerve toxins and have their loved ones ripped away."

"Yes. I want them to watch their homes burn to the ground," Sundew growled. "I want them to feel in their souls what they've done to us."

Swordtail turned to the LeafWing. "I'm in," he said. "Whatever you want me to do. I'll follow you."

Cricket buried her face in her talons. They were right, but they were also wrong. She needed Blue — he was the one who understood dragon hearts. He'd know how to reach them.

All she knew was chemistry and biology and math and botany. How could she stack a pile of scientific logic up against their justifiable anger and hope to convince them?

Wait . . . there was something Blue had said . . .

"The queen," she said suddenly, looking up. "That's it. She's the problem, just like Blue said. We have to start with her."

"Or end with her," Sundew said. "Or get to her in the middle, whenever it's most convenient to set her on fire or bury her alive or feed her to vampire ants."

"No, no, that's what I mean," Cricket said. "Queen Wasp is the heart of the problem, or, like, the brain, I guess. She controls the whole tribe — you saw her do it in the Temple. You'll never have a chance as long as she's out there, inside everyone's minds. And more important, you'll never know which HiveWings might be on your side if they could be."

Swordtail snorted, and Sundew gave him a "right? As if" look.

"They *might* be," Cricket insisted. "Like the Librarian! Remember how she helped us as soon as she was free of Queen Wasp? My sister would, too, if she had the choice. But none of them has a choice right now. If you can shut down the queen's mind control, you'll see who they really are. I think you'll find more allies than you realized you had."

I hope. I hope there are good HiveWings. Clearsight, please let there be good HiveWings underneath what we can see.

"Shut down the mind control," Sundew said thoughtfully. "That would be useful. Is there a way to do that?"

Cricket sighed. "I don't know. I've been looking for an explanation for it practically my whole life. Why doesn't it affect me? Whatever is wrong with me, can we do it to other HiveWings?"

"There's nothing wrong with you," Swordtail said. He sat down by the door, folding his wings back. The orange streaks on his scales reflected the flamesilk glow like distant suns.

"We have to figure out what's right with you and wrong with everyone else in your tribe."

Oh, wow. Maybe he doesn't completely hate me after all.

"Can't the LeafWings do that instead?" Cricket asked Sundew. "Wouldn't it be better to break the mind control instead of starting a new war?"

"It's a very sweet and SilkWingish plan, but how?" Sundew demanded. "Aren't you the smartest dragon around? Who else would know, if you don't?"

Swordtail jumped to his feet and stared at them.

"Yes?" Sundew said when the pause got awkward.

"I'm not sure," he said excitedly. "But I think the Chrysalis has a committee working on this."

"The what?" Sundew said sharply.

He bounced on his talons for a moment, looking torn. "I'm not supposed to tell anyone about them," he said at last. "That was the most important rule. But then Io told Blue and he told you," he said to Cricket. "So . . ."

"He didn't tell me much," she said, remembering the soft brush of her wings against Blue's scales in the dark, the quiet vibration of his voice whispering *Are you with the Chrysalis?* The shiver that had gone down her spine as she wondered what the Chrysalis was, and how many other secrets this beautiful blue dragon knew, and whether he'd stay and tell her everything and be her friend. She'd felt as though she'd just found a new book, something she'd been desperate to read her whole life without even knowing it existed. "I'd really like to know more."

Swordtail hesitated, glancing at Sundew. "I'm sure they'd want to know about the LeafWings . . . but they'd want to know *before* I told you about them. *Arrrrgh.* I wish I knew what Luna would do right now."

"She'd tell us everything," Sundew said promptly.

Cricket laughed, and Sundew gave her a sideways approving glance.

"All right," Swordtail said, nodding at Sundew. "I said I was with you, after all. I think you can change everything for us." He took a deep breath. "The Chrysalis is a secret organization of SilkWings who are fighting for our freedom."

That was exactly the thrilling, stirring answer Cricket had imagined. *Secret freedom fighters in the Hives,* she thought. *Dragons who risk their lives to help others.*

But Sundew looked skeptical. "Fighting?" she said. "SilkWings? Doesn't match."

"Some of us can fight," Swordtail said, bristling. "Some of us care about what's happened to our tribe!"

"What do they do?" Cricket asked. "How do they keep it all secret? I mean, they must be amazing; I've never heard anything about SilkWings fighting back or any kind of underground rebellion."

"Hm," Sundew grunted. "Maybe because they don't actually do anything."

"They do! I'm sure they do. I don't really know what, though." Swordtail shifted on his feet. "My sister and I just joined them recently. We haven't been given a mission or anything yet. They said to wait for further instructions after Luna got her wings. Luna was kind of the main contact person. She's the one who found them."

"But you could find them again?" Sundew demanded.

"I think so," Swordtail said. "Luna could. If I find Luna —"

"Even if you don't," Sundew said, "when Blue comes out of that cocoon, we're going looking for this Chrysalis of yours." She turned to Cricket. "We'll compare their notes and yours and see if we can find an answer to the mind-control thing."

"Thank you," Cricket said.

"Don't get too excited," Sundew warned. "Setting your whole tribe on fire is still my preferred option."

But she listened to me. They both did. There's still a chance I can stop them from starting a new war and save my tribe.

Or at least save Katydid, she thought anxiously.

"So we wait for Blue." Cricket rested her talons on his cocoon, feeling the warmth spread through her scales.

"I'd better go talk to my parents," Sundew said with a sigh. She started looping all the pouches around herself again, wrinkling her snout as the dampest ones squished against her scales. "They're probably wondering where I've disappeared to with the Book. And why I'm letting you lot interfere with my great destiny."

Cricket tilted her head at Sundew. "What great destiny?"

The LeafWing waved her wings expressively. "You know, saving the world, fiery vengeance, so on and so forth. Everything they raised me to do. They are not going to be excited about postponing their war so they can sit around for several days waiting for a SilkWing to wake up."

"Weren't they sitting around in that greenhouse before they met him?" Cricket pointed out. "I thought LeafWings were supposed to be good at acting like great patient trees."

"I'll tell them that," Sundew said with a grin, settling the last pouch in place. "I'm sure it'll help." Cricket noticed with disappointment that Sundew was taking the Book of Clearsight with her. She could understand why, though; the LeafWings had gone to a lot of trouble to get it. They weren't about to leave it in the talons of a HiveWing again, even a HiveWing who'd helped them.

"And I'll go look for Luna again." A piece of seaweed slid free from Swordtail's horns as he glanced out at the stone passageways.

Cricket tried not to look too disappointed that they were both leaving her alone again, after keeping her company for such a short time. The boredom of the quiet cave loomed ahead of her once more.

"Will you be back soon?" she said to Sundew, hoping she didn't sound completely pathetic.

"Yeah, don't worry," Sundew said. "What I do is up to me, not my parents." She hesitated for the briefest moment, like she was about to say something else. "On this mission, anyway."

Cricket wondered what the LeafWing wasn't saying. Was there something in her life that her parents did control? *Maybe Sundew's not as free as she seems to be.*

"Can one of you bring back food?" Cricket asked. "I mean, for Blue? He'll be hungry when he comes out, won't he? After five days in there?"

Swordtail nodded. "I'd never been so hungry," he said. "I'll find something for him."

"What do SilkWings eat?" Sundew said, starting toward the tunnels. "Let me guess: rainbows and honey and starlight."

"Yes to honey, I think," Cricket said. She raised her voice as Sundew's tail disappeared through the gap. "Oh, and while you're out there, if you happen to see any books, I would love something to read!"

She wasn't entirely sure, but something like the sound of Sundew laughing came echoing back from the walls.

— CHAPTER 4 —

"Is it now?" Cricket asked. "Is it happening? Is that a sign? What does that mean?"

"If you don't turn off your beehive brain, I'm going to stick a sleepflower up your snout," Sundew said crossly. "Nothing is happening! It's looked exactly like that all day!" She scowled down at the pouch she'd been trying to mend with a strand of Swordtail's silk.

"No, it hasn't!" Cricket protested, circling Blue's cocoon. "Look, this end is kind of bulging and crinkling. Like it's about to split open! Right, Swordtail? Don't you think so?"

"Sure," he said sleepily, without lifting his head or opening his eyes. She knew he'd spent the last four days flying and searching and scouring every island in Dragonfly Bay, snatching sleep only in brief moments back in the cave. And she knew that not finding Luna was a huge disappointment and they should be very worried and making grave faces and muttering ominously.

But seriously! Blue was about to come out of his cocoon! This was an extremely momentous occasion, mostly because she'd get to see his wonderful face again, but also a little bit because she'd finally get to leave this cave!

"Hey, Blue," she said to the shimmering blue-purple shape beneath the silk. "Can you hear me? We're here. We can't wait to see your wings! I have so many questions. What is it like in there? Do you remember any of it? Is it like a really long sleep? How do your wings feel?"

"FOR THE LOVE OF TREES," Sundew growled. "All right. I was afraid to share this, because I know you're going to *freak out*, but if you promise to be quiet until Blue comes out, I'll tell you about how I saw one of your reading monkeys this morning."

"WHAT?" Cricket nearly flew through the ceiling. "You *did*? Sundew! Really truly? And you're just telling me this now?!" She'd been *so quiet* and careful every time she crept around the caves, hoping to run into one of the tiny creatures. She couldn't believe it was Sundew who'd seen one instead!

"Yes, because of that," Sundew said, pointing at her. "That face you're making, as if I found a staircase to the moons instead of just another weird animal. Calm down, or I won't tell it."

"I'm calm!" Cricket said. She realized she was bouncing on her front talons and forced herself to sit on her tail and stay still. "SO TOTALLY CALM."

"I already regret this," Sundew said. "All right. But NO QUESTIONS."

Cricket clamped her talons over her snout and nodded. Sundew threw the torn leaf pouch across the cave and picked up a bundle of berries, which she started sorting as she talked.

"This morning I went down to the cavern where my parents and I first started digging to Wasp Hive," Sundew started. "I've been checking it regularly to make sure the HiveWings didn't follow our tunnel from the flamesilk cavern. I figured I'd blocked it up pretty well, but safer to be sure."

"How did you bl — oops, sorry," Cricket corrected herself quickly at Sundew's glare.

"Our hole was still completely filled in, but as I scouted the perimeter of the cave, I found another, much smaller hole in the wall. I decided to spy on it for a while in case anything edible came out."

Cricket wasn't sure why she had been surprised to discover that LeafWings were carnivores. It fit with the bloodthirsty, violent picture of them that Queen Wasp painted over the last half century. And yet, in her own heart of hearts, and maybe because of the beautiful drawings of them in the oldest books, she'd somehow imagined a tranquil green tribe sharing sweet potatoes and cranberries across the treetops. So the first time Sundew brought back a pair of headless pigeons and devoured hers in two bites, Cricket had been rather startled. (And vegetarian Swordtail had been openly horrified.)

"Finally," Sundew went on, "I heard a *tip-tap-patter* kind of noise. I squinted at the hole and saw a little head poke out. It was just like the one you described from under the savanna — fluffy black fur on its head, scraps of silver silk and gray fur on its body, hairless long brown paws."

"Perfect for holding books," Cricket breathed.

"This one didn't have a book," Sundew pointed out. "It had a stick with a bit of fire on the end of it."

"Where did — I mean — um, I wish I knew where that came from!" Cricket said quickly. The one she'd seen had had a fire, too. Did the reading monkeys have access to flamesilk somehow?

"Anyway, it saw me, shrieked like a snake-bit panther, and ran away before I could eat it," Sundew said grumpily.

"But you wouldn't have!" Cricket said. "Right? You wouldn't eat something that can *read*, right, Sundew?"

"I'm going to need a little more proof they can do that before I start giving up on prey," Sundew said. "But really I wouldn't eat something you're so completely obsessed with because I know I'd never hear the end of it from you."

"Well, if I have to annoy you into protecting cool new species, then that's what I have to do," Cricket said nobly. "It's so unfair you saw one instead of me! You're so lucky."

Sundew rolled her eyes. "That's me, the luckiest dragon."

A tearing sound came from the cocoon. Swordtail leaped to his feet and joined Cricket, crouching by the end with the rip in it.

"I was right!" she whispered to him. "I knew it was about to happen! It's happening! Do you remember your Metamorphosis? Is there anything we should do when he comes out?"

"Just give him some space," Swordtail said, his wings twitching and his eyes fixed on the shape of claws poking through the silk. "He'll want to breathe for a moment and then eat something." He swept the pile of fruit they'd gathered closer with his tail.

Cricket wished she had her notebook. She'd never seen a Metamorphosis before, and the books were always frustratingly vague about SilkWing details. If she could take notes, maybe one day she could write a paper about what it looked like and how it worked and every step of the process . . .

No. I'll never get to do that. I'm not going to be a published scientist. There's no normal HiveWing life ahead for me.

Unless . . . what if we defeat Queen Wasp? Then what happens?

Could the HiveWings and LeafWings and SilkWings all start living in harmony? Sharing the Hives, planting food, publishing books, going to school together?

Cricket glanced over at Sundew and felt like the weight of one of the moons was settling on her wings.

The LeafWings aren't going to forgive us. How can we ever move on — as though we didn't try to wipe out the LeafWings or dominate the SilkWings?

How can they ever trust us, or want to live alongside us again, after what we've done?

She couldn't imagine a path from Sundew's anger, or her plan to wipe out the HiveWings, to a world in which the three tribes lived in peace. She'd been trying for days, but her thoughts kept circling back to the mind control. As far as she could see, her only hope for avoiding a war was to convince Sundew that HiveWings with free will would be on the LeafWings' side.

Which, if she was honest with herself, she wasn't at all sure of.

A familiar purple snout burst through the silk, shaking filaments off his horns. Cricket held her breath as Blue wriggled and shoved and slid out onto the stone floor, kicking his shredded cocoon away from him. He struggled free and finally stood for a moment with his head bowed, taking deep breaths. And then he looked up, met Cricket's eyes, smiled, and spread his wings.

Cricket wondered if her smile could lift her through the ceiling. Blue's wings were glorious — shimmering purple and blue like sapphires and violets tumbled together. *He* was glorious. She knew she loved more than his beautiful scales and his lovely face — she loved his kindness, and his sweetness, and his sense of humor, and the way he thought about other dragons so deeply, and the fact that he seemed to have no idea at all how handsome he was. But oh my goodness, she also really loved his lovely face.

"Cricket," he said in a hoarse voice. "You stayed."

"Of course I did," she said.

"Thank you," he said, and her heart felt as if it might burst. "I bet that was . . ." He paused and thought for a moment. "Hmm. Boring?"

She laughed. "Just a little."

Can he see how much I adore him? Am I too obvious? I wish I knew what he feels.

Swordtail stepped forward and offered a leaf cup full of water. Blue took it gratefully and drank the whole thing.

"Nice wings," Swordtail observed. "Not as handsome as mine, of course, but pretty cool. See, I told you Metamorphosis wasn't that bad."

Blue flicked his friend's tail with his own. "I can't believe it's over," he said. "After all those years of worrying about it!" He stretched his wings as wide as they would go and wrinkled his snout as though he was trying to stop smiling. "Remember how Luna and I were waiting for you when you came out?"

"With a giant box of honey drops and Luna's weird banana mash cake," Swordtail said, grinning.

"You did a really good job of pretending to like it," Blue said. He studied his wings, which looked shiny and damp in a brand-new kind of way. "I guess the one upside of being fugitives is she can't make one of those for me." His eyes searched the cave. "Hey, Sundew."

"Hey yourself, SilkWing," Sundew said gruffly. "You sure took your time growing those flappers." Cricket wondered whether Blue could tell that the LeafWing was actually happy to see him, or whether it was only Cricket who was getting used to the mostly hidden expressions under Sundew's scowls. "So are you actually a flamesilk? Can you make fire?"

"I feel like I can." Blue held out his talons and glowing flame spiraled from each wrist into smoking curls of light on the floor. Sundew inspected them, nodded approvingly, and scooped them into a small stone jar from one of her pouches.

While she did that, Blue took a short, shuddering breath and looked at Swordtail, and by the expression on his face, Cricket could tell that he'd already guessed the worst. "Luna," he said anxiously.

"I'm sorry, Blue," Swordtail said, his wings drooping. "I can't find her. I've looked and looked."

Blue was quiet for a long moment. Cricket took a step closer to those iridescent wings and gently twined her tail around his. He seemed so much bigger, suddenly.

"If you haven't found her," Blue said, "then she must still be alive. We'd feel it if she wasn't, don't you think? Maybe she's hiding somewhere and hasn't made it back yet. She'll find us again. I'm sure she will, Swordtail. She's probably out there worrying about us twice as much as we're worrying about her."

"Well, she's not finding us here," Sundew said, standing up. She dropped her sorted berries into sections of a leaf bag and put it on, then started assembling all her other pouches around her in some careful order Cricket hadn't mapped out yet. "We've already stayed way too long. It's a miracle the HiveWings searching the coast haven't found us yet."

"It's not a miracle," Swordtail said. "It's you. You hid the entrance to this tunnel really well. I've seen HiveWing guards walk right past it as they hunt through the cave. I've gotten lost like eight times coming back from the bay, because it's so hard to spot." He handed Blue a talonful of kumquats and sliced yams. "I don't know how she did it. Wait until you see what she did with the vines and the moss . . . it's kind of amazing."

Sundew made the face she always made when Cricket or Swordtail said something nice about her, as though her expressions had no practice reacting to compliments, so they just threw out a few spasms and then went back to scowling. "Well, it won't last forever," she said. "Let's get to a Hive and find the Chrysalis."

"The Chrysalis?" Blue echoed between bites, looking at Swordtail.

"We'll explain on the way," Cricket offered.

"So, what — back to Wasp Hive?" Sundew asked.

Blue shuddered. "Um . . . is that our only option?"

"It's not the best place to find the Chrysalis," Swordtail said. "I mean, it's the most dangerous Hive. Swarming with soldiers. I'm not even sure they have any members there."

Sundew gave him a hard look. "I thought you said they were in all the Hives."

"I *think* they are," he said. "But let's try another one, just to be safe, is my suggestion."

"Where are we, exactly?" Cricket said. She took Sundew's discarded leaf pouch, flattened out one side of it, and sliced a rough map of Pantala into the thick pale green surface with her claws. "We came from Wasp Hive, up here." She stabbed a little hole in the spot where Wasp Hive would be on the map.

"Kind of here," Swordtail said, pointing to a spot on the coast of Dragonfly Bay, a ways south of Wasp Hive.

"So let's think. The next closest Hives are these three." Cricket poked three holes in the map. "Yellowjacket Hive, Bloodworm Hive . . . or Jewel Hive." She hesitated, feeling an old familiar twist like thorns around her heart.

"What is it?" Blue asked, touching her shoulder. "Why does Jewel Hive make you sad?"

"It's — nothing really," she said. "Just, that's where my mother moved, when she left us."

Cricket could remember that day really clearly. She'd been three years old; Katydid had been twelve, but still living at home and without a partner, chosen or assigned.

It had felt completely out of the blue to her, like a Hive suddenly collapsing for no reason. Mother had been standing with all her belongings at the door when they returned from school, her books being loaded into baskets by a pair of sturdy SilkWings. She'd looked faintly annoyed that they'd returned before she could disappear. Katydid had cried, but Cricket couldn't — it was all too confusing. She didn't understand why they couldn't continue as they always did, with her mother ignoring them all. Why did she have to go to a whole other Hive to do that?

"I didn't know your mother left," Blue said sympathetically.

"That's not an option for SilkWings," Swordtail pointed out. "At least, not by choice. Nobody gets to leave the partner they're paired with, unless Queen Wasp tells them to."

"HiveWings have to get her approval first," Cricket said. "I guess Mother *really* wanted to get away from us if she was willing to go through the whole separation request process. When she left, she said, 'Across the continent still isn't far enough from you horrible grubs, but it'll have to do.'"

"Whoa." Sundew hissed through her teeth. "She sounds charming."

"Oh, Cricket," Blue said. "How could anyone say that to her own dragonets?"

"She'd been trying to leave for a while, it turns out," Cricket said, fiddling with the edge of the leaf. "But I mean, it doesn't matter. It's not like we'll run into her — it's a big Hive, super busy. I kind of know my way around from the two times we visited her, so maybe that'll be helpful."

Blue rested one of his wings alongside hers, like a warm azure wave of comfort if she wanted it. She liked that he didn't push her to talk about it more.

"What's the plan?" she asked Sundew. "How do we get into the Hive if everyone's looking for us?"

"With punching and biting?" Swordtail suggested hopefully. "And maybe some venomous caterpillars?"

"I like the way you think," Sundew said. "But they're centipedes, dingbat."

"Or," Blue interjected, "is there a way to sneak in where nobody gets hurt?"

"And nobody gets caught by HiveWing guards," Cricket agreed. She looked down at her map again. "Jewel Hive. Hmmm."

"What what what?" Sundew demanded.

"Lady Jewel is a little different from the other Hive rulers," Cricket explained. "Do you guys know anything about her? She's Wasp's cousin, not her sister, for one thing. And she's famous for her . . . I guess 'love of art' is the best way to describe it?"

"Oh, right!" Swordtail said, lighting up. "Luna was always talking about how she wanted to move to Jewel Hive if we could! She kept going on about the art scene and the Glitterbazaar." The light went out of his eyes and he looked down at his claws. "She would love to see the Glitterbazaar."

"Maybe the Chrysalis will know something," Blue said to him. "Maybe she found her way to them, or maybe they'd know if she's back in the flamesilk cavern."

Swordtail looked hopeful for the first time in days. "That's true! If she ended up in a Hive, that's who she'd look for!" He flicked his tail back and forth. "We should go ask them! Let's do that! Let's go now!"

"Hang on, what in Pantala is a Glitterbazaar?" Sundew asked. "If it involves sparkles, the answer is no. I do *not* do sparkles." Which was funny, Cricket thought, coming from a dragon with gold flecks all across her green scales.

"Only a few sparkles," Cricket said, "and I think it might be our way in . . ."

CHAPTER 5

Cricket hadn't realized how nerve-racking it must have been for Swordtail and Sundew to creep out of the cave onto the beach every day. You couldn't get a full view of the sky until you were already exposed on the sand. If HiveWings had been watching from the cliffs, they would have spotted her friends easily, even at night, with the moons lighting up the ocean.

Raindrops pattered against her scales and blurred her glasses as she stepped into the open air for the first time in days, keeping her body close to the towering cliff face. They were lucky tonight. Dark clouds covered most of the three moons, driving rain obscured the sky, and the fierce thunderstorm was probably keeping most HiveWing scouts at home.

Of course, it meant flying to Jewel Hive in that very thunderstorm, but Cricket for one would rather battle the rain than another dragon.

"Bleh. Pffft. Ugh," Swordtail muttered, shaking wet sand off his talons and snout. "Sorry your first flying experience has to be in this weather, Blue."

"It's amazing," Blue said. "I mean, from down here." He lifted his face up to the rain and held out his faintly glowing wrists. Skittering rivulets ran like melted amethysts along his wings. She wasn't imagining it; his wings were decidedly larger than Cricket's. It was a little intimidating, until he turned and smiled at Cricket. His smile was still the same; it still took up just as much space in her heart.

I'm such a moon-moth. Didn't I laugh at dragons who said things like that in my books? You don't even know if he likes you back, because he seems to be just that sweet to everybody.

Seriously, Cricket, snap to it. You're trying to save your tribe and avoid all-out war right now. And if Swordtail is right about the Chrysalis, you could be this close *to solving your brain chemistry mystery.*

"Lead the way," Sundew said, nudging Cricket. "I'll watch for HiveWings. Swordtail, you keep an eye on Blue and his new wings."

"Will do," Swordtail said solemnly.

It was a shaky flight, punctuated by earsplitting thunder and crackling bolts of lightning overhead. The rain battered Cricket's wings and blurred her glasses and flew into her eyes so she could hardly keep track of the coastline below her. She was very, very glad that they didn't have far to go.

She knew her job was to lead the way to Jewel Hive, but she couldn't help twisting around to keep an eye on Blue every few heartbeats. It was hard enough flying for the first time, let alone doing it in a thunderstorm.

The first time she'd flown in the rain, it had been a training exercise at Terrarium Academy. And it had been *very* annoying, not because of the weather, but because of her classmate Bombardier. He was completely convinced that Cricket had a crush on him and was always trying to "let her down gently," when in fact Cricket would have very much liked to throw him through a wall.

She remembered trying to figure out how to flick raindrops off her back wings. Bombardier kept hovering around her, offering unnecessary suggestions.

"I can figure it out myself," she'd finally snapped at him.

"You don't need to act self-confident with me," he'd answered condescendingly. "It won't make me like you more, Cricket. I keep telling you, I'm not interested in you that way."

"Neither am I!" she'd tried to protest, like she always did.

"Of course, of course," he'd soothed her insincerely, and then smug-faced away while she wished she had *any* cool HiveWing powers to poison him with.

Blue was the furthest opposite dragon from Bombardier that Cricket had ever met. He had no idea how wonderful he was, and he would never assume that somebody liked him. He always really wanted to know what other dragons were feeling, no matter who they were.

He seemed to have less trouble with the storm than she'd feared. His wings looked so new and shimmering that she kept thinking the wind would tear them right in half, but Blue beat them strongly and smoothly, as though he'd been flying forever. Every time she turned to look at him, he gave her his shy smile, as though she had something to do with the wind that lifted his wings.

Oh, Blue. I won't let them use you to hurt any dragons. We'll figure out the mind control and stop Queen Wasp, and then you can use your flamesilk to make the world a better place instead of worse.

Soon she could see the glowing lights of Jewel Hive up ahead. Flamesilk lanterns lit many of the windows, and as they flew closer, she caught glimpses of a bright party taking place on one of the upper levels. Dragons laughed and danced and whirled, orange-gold scales and green jewels flashing through a ballroom hung with vibrant scarlet and cobalt silk tapestries.

Cricket remembered hiding on the edges of that ballroom while her mother danced, at a party neither she nor Katydid had wanted to be dragged to. But her mother never missed one of Lady Jewel's parties, her best chance to get closer to the ruler of her new Hive. Katydid had found a bubbly drink for them to share that tasted like limes and made Cricket sleepy. The wasps on the tapestries had been dyed a gold so bright it hurt her eyes.

She missed Katydid. When Cricket flew off with Blue, she hadn't expected to be gone for so long. She hadn't thought about the possibility that she'd never be able to go home again . . . that she might never see her sister again.

But I'd still have gone, even knowing all that. I think I had to.

They arced around Jewel Hive and landed a fair distance away, farther out on the peninsula, at the top of a cliff where they could hear the sound of waves roaring below even through the storm. Somehow, standing out in the rain felt even harder than flying, as though the raindrops were trying to beat Cricket into the earth.

"So there's the Hive," Sundew shouted to Swordtail. "Where do we go to find the Chrysalis?"

Cricket wasn't great at reading dragons' expressions, but she thought Swordtail looked decidedly nervous as he answered, "Well, we don't exactly find them. We leave them a message and they find us."

"Leave them a message how?" Cricket asked. "Where?"

"Um." He shook his wings and tail. "So. I'm kind of . . . guessing? I mean, I sort of know, but I wasn't going to be the one who . . . I mean, I'm just saying, this would be a lot easier if Luna were here."

"But she's not," Sundew said. "Not yet," she amended at the look on his face. "You have to figure this out, SilkWing. We can't wait for her."

"Wait, why not?" Blue asked. "Can't we go hide somewhere new for a few days until we find her and then decide what to do?"

The grass was soggy and felt like dense wet carpet under Cricket's claws. She blinked away raindrops and looked at Sundew.

"No!" Sundew said. "We've *been* waiting for *you*, you snoozy SilkWing." She turned to Cricket. "My parents can't put their plans on hold forever."

Lightning flickered deep in the clouds, reflecting waves of green fire in the ocean. Cricket felt the tremor of thunder rumble through her bones.

"What does that mean?" Cricket asked. "What plans? How long do you think they'll wait?"

Sundew huffed and ripped up a muddy tuft of grass, then carefully tucked it back into the divot she'd made and covered it with her claws. "All right," she said. "Two days."

"Two *days*?" Cricket cried. "That's it? That's all the time we have to solve the entire mystery of Queen Wasp's mind control?"

"Or what?" Blue asked anxiously. "What happens in two days?"

"That's all I could get!" Sundew shouted back at Cricket. "I tried, all right? It was almost impossible! It was like — like trying to push a tree back up when it's already started falling. Belladonna and Hemlock don't think you can do it. So I'm sorry, but if I don't have some kind of results for them by sunset in two days, they're going to the next phase of their plan."

"What are they going to do?" Cricket asked. Blue looked paler and paler with each of her questions. "Are they going to attack a Hive? Will it restart the Tree Wars? What plan, Sundew?"

"The LeafWing plan that is not for HiveWings to know about," Sundew said sternly. "But it involves violence and you're not going to like it as much as *this* plan, so we should get *moving* on this plan in order to make sure that it's the one that works. Understand?"

Swordtail nodded.

"Restart the Tree Wars?" Blue whispered, nearly drowned out by the storm.

Cricket's heart was beating very fast. She wanted to know the LeafWing plan; she wanted to know how many LeafWings were out there and where they would attack and whether Katydid would be in danger.

But the only thing she did know was she wouldn't get those answers out of Sundew by asking for them now.

And at least she had a chance. Two days. Two days to find the answers and stop the LeafWings.

"All right," she said, trying to steady her breathing. "We can do this. Let's think. Swordtail, where do you need to get to so you can leave a message for the Chrysalis?"

"A central feature," he said. "In Cicada Hive, it was the Salvation mosaic in the Mosaic Garden. Does — does Jewel Hive have a Salvation mosaic?"

"No." Cricket shook her head.

He looked worried. "Does it have anything like that?"

Cricket bowed her head and tried to think. Her visits to her mother hadn't exactly involved fun tours of awesome Hive monuments. But maybe there was an answer in something she'd read . . . Her mind started ticking through books about other Hives, monuments to the Salvation, architecture and unifying features, the history of Hive-building, Wasp's sisters and Lady Jewel . . .

"There's the statue in the center of the Glitterbazaar," she said slowly. "That's a tribute to the Salvation. Or there's a garden at the top of the Hive, like the Mosaic Garden. It doesn't have mosaics or historical monuments, but it has a wading pool and a shrine to Clearsight."

"The garden," Swordtail said.

"The statue," Sundew said at the same time.

"Really?" he said to her. "I'd think it would be in roughly the same place, like, geographically. Don't you?"

"No, *my* revolution would be organized around the symbolism," she said. "If it's in a meaningful place in one Hive, I'd guess the Chrysalis in the next Hive would choose a place with the same meaning."

"Hm." Swordtail rubbed his face, trying unsuccessfully to dry it. "I don't know. I don't know. I wish —"

"Luna were here, yes, we know," Sundew said. "OK, here's what we do. Leave a message in both places. Hope the Chrysalis finds one of them."

"And the HiveWings don't," Blue said.

"It'll be easiest to go to the Glitterbazaar first," Cricket suggested. She pointed down toward Jewel Hive, at the dark shapes that sprawled in a scattered tangle around the bottom of it. "We start on the outskirts, get our disguises, and work our way in."

And pray to Clearsight that we can do this in two days.

CHAPTER 6

The next morning dawned gray and drizzly, but at least the pouring rain had moved out along with the apocalyptic thunder. One half of Cricket was cold and damp when she woke up, but the side that had been pressed to Blue while they slept was warm.

He was still asleep, like a small sunlit ocean between her and Swordtail. She put on her glasses and looked up at the thick silk web over them, and then around for Sundew, who was gone.

Carefully Cricket disentangled her tail from Blue's and slid away from his wings. He murmured a sleepy complaint and rolled closer to Swordtail, who grunted and flung one wing over him.

The silk web overhead was part of a vast canopy that covered all the stalls of the outer bazaar — the lowlier shops that had spilled out of the Hive when the Glitterbazaar got too big. It wasn't great to have your stall outside the Hive during the rainy season, but at least the canopy helped keep the wares mostly dry.

They'd hidden overnight in the musty-smelling back corners of a curtain shop, burrowing in between rolls of aquamarine and silver silk. Cricket crawled out of the fabric pile and ducked into the main stall. A web hung over the doorway, keeping out most of the dim morning light, but a flamesilk lamp glowed softly in one corner. Sundew was stretching in the tiny space.

"Morning," Cricket said. She sidled up and joined Sundew's series of exercises, like she had each morning in the cave. It was a little harder here, trying to keep her wings from colliding with Sundew's.

"When do the dragons come?" Sundew asked, finishing her last stretch. She peeked out through the door web at the Hive, looming in the mist.

"Jewel Hive sleeps late," Cricket said apologetically. "The balls sometimes go all night. We won't see many HiveWings before midday. Are all LeafWings early risers, like you?"

"Some of them. This market must open sooner, though." Sundew checked back in the other direction, along the path through the stalls. "Aren't some of these places run by SilkWings?"

"Most of the ones on the outside are," Cricket said,

nodding. "We should find what we need now and then blend in with the crowd once it's busy enough."

Sundew cast a wicked smile at the back of the shop. "I'll wake the others!" she volunteered, bounding away.

A moment later, Cricket heard Swordtail yelp, "Ow! Unnecessary!" followed by the unusual sound of Sundew laughing.

Cricket took a moment to peer out into the market as well. She'd walked through it with Katydid once, but she didn't know the layout at all. Was there an order to the stalls? Were they organized together by category of item they sold, or scattered wherever they'd happened to land?

From what she knew of Jewel Hive, she'd guess scattered, and she'd also guess that there wasn't a map anywhere in the market, if one had ever even been made. Lady Jewel wasn't exactly known for keeping her subjects organized.

Which is good for us. This is probably the Hive where we have the best chance of going unnoticed, between the chaos of the dragons who live here and the undisciplined guards.

Then again, there wasn't really anywhere they could go unnoticed if Queen Wasp decided to take over the eyes of every dragon in Pantala.

But it had been five days since Luna and Blue escaped the flamesilk cavern. Cricket was hoping the search for them might have quieted down, at least a little bit.

Blue and Swordtail emerged from the back of the stall, yawning, with Sundew behind them looking mischievously pleased.

"You really take an unholy amount of pleasure in ripping happy dragons out of their peaceful slumbers," Swordtail said to her.

"It's the best part of my day," she said. "A little tiny bit of vengeance every morning."

Blue's expression went slightly trancelike, as though he'd slipped into a cloud of trying to imagine what it was like to be Sundew.

"We should hurry," Cricket whispered. "I'm not sure how long we have before the first SilkWings arrive — and I don't know how long it'll take to find what we want in this place. It's bigger than I remember."

They ducked under the door web and Cricket led the way along the narrow, cluttered paths of the market. All the stalls had their door webs or curtains lowered, but it was easy to tell what they sold by the merchandise that spilled over the edges and hung from the frames. The group passed an instrument stall with zebra-hide drums and curved black metal harps. The next had a sign listing a selection of fruit juices, and the one after that featured curious flamesilk lanterns (without the flamesilk) shaped like snails or leopards or birds in flight.

Totally disorganized, Cricket thought. *Each stall dropped wherever the shop owner could grab a space under the canopy.* It was unhelpful for their search, but also kind of wonderfully free. Everything in Cicada Hive was regimented and orderly in a way that Cricket had never quite fit into. She wondered if her life would have been easier growing up in Jewel Hive. She also wondered how her inflexible mother could stand it.

"Oh, there!" she cried, spotting a flare of bright silk poking out under a curtain. They hurried over and she pushed through into the dark stall. Her eyes adjusted slowly. There were no flamesilk lamps in here, or at least, if there were, they were empty. Cricket squinted at the silk draped and folded on the shelves. It was hard to see any colors or details with the outer stall curtains down.

"Here," Blue whispered. He held out one talon, and a small twist of silk spiraled out of his wrist onto his palm. It glowed there like a miniature comet caught in his claws, lighting up the room.

"So cool." Swordtail leaned toward it and Blue moved it out of his reach.

"Careful. This will burn. I'm the only one who can touch it safely."

"Flamesilk doesn't burn you?" Cricket asked, surprised. "Even the kind in the lanterns?" How had she missed that in her reading?

"My dad said it wouldn't, after my Metamorphosis." Blue lifted the light toward the ceiling so it illuminated all the colors around them. "And this is the kind in the lanterns."

"So be careful with it," Sundew said. "Or else you'll set this whole place on fire. And maybe the Hive, too," she added thoughtfully. "On second thought, go ahead and wave it around."

Cricket realized a few moments later that she should have been appalled by that joke, but she was distracted by the thought of how much she didn't know about flamesilk. She wished she could stop for a day to investigate all the different kinds of flamesilk Blue could make now and what they could each do.

But we only have until sunset tomorrow to stop a new war. Fascinating scientific experiments would have to wait.

"I think this is what we want," she said, tugging a waterfall of sunflower-yellow silk off the wall. She flung it over Sundew's shoulders. The LeafWing was the one who'd stand out the most of all of them. Her forest-green scales might pass for a SilkWing's at a glance, but those two wings screamed "LEAFWING! ARREST ME!"

The silk draped along Sundew's back and halfway down her tail, covering her wings and most of her body. Sundew twisted her neck to give it a suspicious look.

"What is this?" she asked. "What self-respecting dragon would wear something that would tangle up their wings like this?"

"It's a cape," Cricket said patiently, tying the ribbons around Sundew's neck and arranging the folds to cover her shoulders. "My mother thought they were very fashionable last time I saw her."

"Oh, good, a dragon we already know has excellent judgment," Sundew muttered.

"If you keep your wings folded in close," Swordtail said, squinting at her, "and nobody accidentally pulls it off or peeks underneath . . . I'm still not sure it'll work."

"Could a SilkWing afford something like this?" Blue asked, touching one of the garments with his free talon. "And she doesn't have antennae."

"Also, it's a little bright," Sundew said. "If I must wear something ridiculous, I'd prefer it in black or dark green or midnight blue if absolutely necessary."

"Nope," Cricket said, swatting Sundew's talons away from the nearest dark-colored silk. "In Jewel Hive, everyone is devoted to bright colors, lots of jewels, accessories everywhere. That's the only reason I think we have a chance of sneaking in. It's hard to notice anyone if everyone is trying to stand out . . . unless we slink around in black, looking boring. We have to match the glamour around us."

"Even the SilkWings?" Blue asked.

"Yes," Cricket said. "There's an ongoing competition here for who can hire the prettiest SilkWing. Some of them don't even have to do anything except sit in parlors and windows and porches and balconies being beautiful."

Swordtail growled softly. "Dragons as decoration."

"Maybe some of them like it?" Blue offered. "It sounds easier than smashing and remolding treestuff all day."

"It sounds mind-numbing," Sundew snorted. "You couldn't pay *me* to have a bunch of HiveWings stare at me all day long."

Cricket privately agreed with her. She could only imagine sitting still for that long if she had a really interesting book to read.

"Well, sorry, that's what you have to be for today," Cricket said. "A very fancy SilkWing." She turned back to the other silks, wishing she knew how much detail Queen Wasp had given out in the search for them. Did they all have to wear wing-covering capes? Were veils still in fashion? Cricket knew almost nothing about accessories; they were frowned upon at Terrarium Academy.

She found two smaller capes for Swordtail and Blue, in matching shades of rose gold with sparkling indigo beetles embroidered all over them. Her hope was to have them all look so bright and busy that no one's eyes would be able to completely land on them — or notice the scales underneath.

"These are kind of cool," Blue said, sliding a basket over to her. Inside were several translucent scarves and arm sheaths woven with glittering black markings.

"Oh, wow," Cricket said, pulling one over her forearm. It looked like the glittering markings were part of her scales, as though she had extra lines and zigzags of black over and around her natural inkblot patches. If she wore several of these on her legs, tail, and neck, she would look more like a black dragon with spots of yellow and orange than vice versa, which would hopefully make it harder to recognize her. She pulled out a few more and started putting them on.

"How are we going to pay for all this?" Blue asked.

"You eternally sweet idiot," Swordtail said, poking him in the side. "We're already on the run from the law, remember? So who cares if we steal a few capes? We can't get in any more trouble than we already are."

Blue winced. "I know. But that's not . . . it's just, some dragon worked hard on all this, and they probably need the money for their family. It's wrong to steal from them."

"Oh . . . that," Swordtail said with a sigh.

"Well, I hope someone's hiding a small fortune under one of your wings, then," Sundew said wryly.

"I guess we could leave those two yams I dug up yesterday," Swordtail said with a wistful expression.

"Your cape is probably worth a hundred yams," Cricket admitted.

"WHAT?" Swordtail protested. "This silly thing? It doesn't even do anything! Why's it so expensive? Is it edible?"

"How much is flamesilk worth?" Blue asked. "Could I leave them this?" He held out the strand of fire.

Cricket hesitated. "Yes . . . flamesilk is pretty expensive. That would cover all of this, I think, especially since it's brand-new and should last them a whole moon cycle. But, Blue, someone will figure out it had to be you who left it, don't you think? Who else would have bright new flamesilk like that?"

"Maybe someone ordered it from Wasp Hive, like your school librarian does," Blue said. "It feels like the right thing to do."

"Arrgh, you are such a *SilkWing*," Sundew groaned. "This is the *worst* idea. It's basically leaving evidence behind."

"No one will guess it's from the little dragonet who ran away from Cicada Hive," Blue said. He slipped the strand into the lantern on the ceiling, and light filled the stall. "It could have come from any early morning customer." He paused and rubbed his wrists with a small smile. "It's kind of awesome knowing I have something everyone needs. I could give it away to anyone, anytime I want."

"*Or,*" Swordtail observed, "you could *set your enemies on fire* anytime you want."

Sundew pointed one claw at Swordtail. "You," she said, "are growing on me."

Blue shook his head and met Cricket's eyes with a faintly sick expression. She guessed he was trying to imagine being a dragon who could set another living creature on fire, and that it was beyond his abilities. She brushed one of his wings with hers. *I like you as you are, the dragon who gifts fire to those who need it.*

"This stall is just silk," Cricket said, glancing around. "Come on, we need some jewelry, too."

"Jeeeeeewwwwwwwwelry," Sundew complained. But even she had to admit, a little while later in a shrouded jewelry stall, that the long necklaces of little gold leaves Cricket found were kind of cool and she'd maybe be all right with wearing just one of them.

She was less pleased with Cricket's other discovery, the thing Cricket had really been looking for: a gold-and-jade headdress with so many points and squiggles and sparkles that it hid the fact that Sundew had no antennae. The LeafWing carried on as though Cricket was attaching actual snakes to her head, but the end result was quite dazzling and entirely distracting.

"This is the WORST," Sundew grumbled, glaring into a mirror. "Wil — my tribe would fall over *laughing* at me right now."

"I'm sure they'd understand that sometimes you have to sacrifice your dignity for a higher purpose," Swordtail joked.

Sundew swatted at him and he darted out of the way.

In the same stall, they found bejeweled head coverings for Blue and Swordtail that hung like masks of dewdrops around their eyes, and a bright blue veil-shawl-tiara-thing that mostly hid Cricket's face and glasses, plus was also gaudy enough that Sundew was a little mollified.

"At least I'm not the only one who looks like an exploding peony," she said, surveying the others.

"I'm surprised these are allowed," Blue said to Cricket, trailing his claws along the dangling leaves that ornamented a row of bracelets. "I would have thought leaves fit under the rules against trees."

"Maybe in Cicada Hive. Lady Jewel allows her dragons to fly a little closer to the edges of the rules than most Hive leaders," Cricket pointed out.

"What rules against trees?" Sundew asked sharply.

"We, um." Blue faltered under her outraged glare. "We're forbidden to put any trees in our art. No tree sculptures, no trees in the background of our paintings."

"No planting trees in our terrariums," Cricket said, thinking wistfully of her secret little tree, back at school. Would anyone take care of it now that she was gone? "Some fruit trees are allowed in the greenhouses, but only with special permission and strictly under supervision by Queen Wasp. No tree planting or anything that might make a tree grow in the savanna."

Sundew picked up a rope of pearls, wound it around her front talons, and snapped the cord with one violent tug. Pearls flew everywhere, clattering over the countertops.

"Let's go," she growled at Cricket. With a whirl of her saffron silk cape, she stalked out into the market.

"Whoa," Swordtail said, looking up from a basket of turquoise earrings near the back of the stall. "Did she just get even angrier, or did I imagine that?"

"Definitely angrier," Cricket said. "I don't know why, though. Do you, Blue?"

"I think . . . I think maybe erasing trees even from our art is like Queen Wasp trying to wipe out the LeafWings all over again," Blue said. "I mean, maybe that's how it feels to Sundew."

"I never thought of it like that," Cricket said. She'd always thought it was a silly rule; trees were just another plant, and plants were useful for lots of things, and why not have more if they could? She'd never seen them as a symbol of the long-gone LeafWings, but now she realized that Queen Wasp must think of them that way.

Blue left three little coils of flamesilk in a stone vase on the counter and ducked outside with Swordtail. As Cricket started to follow them, she heard a small clattering sound behind her.

Probably a mouse, she told herself, but she edged back toward the counter with her heart thumping. If there was another dragon in here, who'd seen them putting on their disguises, or Blue creating flamesilk from his wrists . . .

The baskets of jewelry behind the counter were still and quiet. Nobody could possibly be hiding back there; there weren't any corners or shadows big enough for a dragon.

But then something moved — something darted from one basket to another. Something smaller than a dragon, but bigger than a mouse. Something with dark fur and swift paws.

A reading monkey!

I really need a better name for them.

Cricket leaned over the counter, staring at the basket where it had disappeared. A long moment passed, and then a small head poked out and stared back at her. Alert brown eyes. A sweet face, narrower than a monkey's and furless except for the top of its head.

"Don't be afraid," Cricket said softly. "I just want to know what you are."

The creature gazed at her. Was that curiosity in its eyes? Did it want to understand her, too?

"Cricket!" Swordtail shouted, sticking his head back into the stall. The little animal jumped and vanished behind the baskets. "Dragons are coming from the Hive!"

Oh, why couldn't I have found one of you before all this started happening? Cricket cast one last longing look at the creature's hiding spot and then turned to hurry outside.

Swordtail was right. Dragons were starting to spill out of the Hive's doors and flying ledges, swooping off into the sky or down toward the market. Jewel Hive was waking up for the day, or at least its SilkWings were.

The tricky part was keeping out of sight until the market was relatively crowded. They managed by moving between stalls and staying in the corners of the ones Cricket guessed were run by HiveWings, and so more likely to open later. There was a close call with a SilkWing who was sweeping behind the tents, but soon the narrow pathways were full of dragons.

Cricket breathed a sigh of relief. She'd been right about Jewel Hive; her memories hadn't failed her. Everyone wore bright colors and piles of gemstones. Capes swirled beside wings everywhere and headdresses glittered from half of the heads around them. Even the SilkWings who swept the streets had adornments in their ears or silk scarves around their necks.

They edged through the crowd, making their way slowly toward the Hive. Cricket tried to look as though she was shopping, pausing to examine the merchandise here and there, smiling faintly at the stall owners who tried to lure her inside.

She was the only HiveWing in the group, so most dragons would assume the other three were her SilkWing servants. It was weird and uncomfortable to have them trailing behind her, heads down. It made her feel guilty to think about how many times she'd walked past their own SilkWing cook without saying hello or taken the SilkWing workers at the market for granted.

She wished Sundew could lead the way. She wished Blue could walk alongside her, wing to wing, so she could laugh with him and talk to him and let everyone know he was wonderful and just as important and interesting and valuable as any HiveWing dragon in Pantala.

But she kept up her part, acting like any other self-absorbed, fashion-obsessed HiveWing in Jewel Hive. Soon the main doors of the Hive were ahead of them, swarming with dragons coming in and out of the central Glitterbazaar, which occupied the bottom three levels of the city. All the windows were open to let in the sun, and the streets and stalls ahead of them shone like a shattered frozen rainbow.

Behind her, Sundew cleared her throat meaningfully. Cricket glanced around and noticed the HiveWing guards posted on either side of the doors. They wore sleek black armor and helmets that hid their faces, but Cricket guessed that the eyes glaring through the little slits would be dead white.

Cricket felt a shiver of terrified despair.

Queen Wasp was watching. Queen Wasp was everywhere. At the entrance to every Hive, flying patrols over the savanna, inside every HiveWing if she wanted to be.

How could they possibly hope to sneak by her? How could they ever escape, when her gaze and her fury could follow them wherever they went?

The closest guard turned his head sharply toward them.

— CHAPTER 7 —

"Don't look at them. Don't react," Sundew whispered fiercely, stepping on Cricket's tail. Cricket turned toward her with what she hoped was a lofty HiveWing expression. This had the added benefit of curving her head away from the guard who was staring at them.

"It's all so *boring*," Cricket said in the high, slow way that Jewel Hive dragons often talked. "I feel like I've seen *everything* a million times. Where's the *originality*, I mean, *yawn*."

"You should try Raindrop Scales," a HiveWing beside her in the crowd interjected unexpectedly. "They're only open during the rainy season so everything feels brand-new! I *love* them. Have you heard of Pinacate? She's the owner and the designer. She has a trillion innovative ideas every year; it's incredible. I wish I were that creative!"

"Wow, really? I don't think I've been there," Cricket said, surprised into using her real voice. The stranger was a summer-squash-yellow color with flecks of red and black scales and black wings, but she'd covered herself with webs of garnets and what Cricket guessed were fake diamonds, since there were so many of them. A long sea-green silk scarf was wound around her neck and body, all the way down her tail, pinned together with an enormous dragonfly brooch on her back.

"It's right by the Salvation Statue," the other dragon confided. "Very expensive, though. I must admit I often go there for ideas and then see if I can find someone to imitate them. Don't tell." She giggled in a warm, friendly way.

"Your secret is safe with me," Cricket said, smiling back at her.

But the reverse would not be true, she thought with a twinge of anxiety. The HiveWing was all smiles and stories now, but if this dragon discovered that Cricket was a fugitive, wouldn't she turn her in immediately? Or, even if she understood and wanted to help them, she wouldn't be able to, because at any moment Queen Wasp could steal her mind. This other HiveWing could never choose to run away like Cricket had; she could never be free of the queen. She didn't have the choice to think for herself.

She'd helped them inadvertently, though. Cricket snuck a sideways peek at the guards. The one who'd looked over must have seen two HiveWings gossiping and lost interest;

he was now staring attentively at the movement of birds on the canopy.

"Thank you very much," Cricket said to the yellow dragon as they stepped inside. "I mean — um, for the recommendation."

"Maybe I'll see you there!" the HiveWing chirped. She waved and bustled away.

The walls around them were weirdly both comforting and claustrophobic. Cricket was so used to living in a Hive, with walls around her all the time. And yet she found her scales prickling anxiously, her eyes wishing for the sky overhead.

It's not the walls that are bothering me, she acknowledged to herself. *It's the dragons inside them.*

"She seemed really nice," Blue whispered as they wound their way toward the center of the market.

"For a HiveWing," Sundew scoffed.

"She did seem nice," Cricket agreed, keeping her voice low. "That's the kind of dragon I'm talking about, Sundew. What would she do if the queen didn't control her? I mean — if she knew the truth about everything — the flamesilks, the Book of Clearsight — and she didn't have the queen in her head, making her do things and messing with her thoughts. Then could we trust her? Maybe she would try to help us."

"Like you," Blue said. "Maybe she'd be like you. Maybe a lot of them wish they could be free."

"Doubtful," Sundew said. "Everything is easy for HiveWings like her. Why would she risk her own happy life?"

"Yeah," Swordtail said fervently. "HiveWings don't care about anyone but themselves."

Cricket flinched, and Blue frowned at Swordtail. "That's really unfair, Swordtail. You don't know what's going on in their hearts. The only HiveWing you know well is Cricket, and she cares a lot."

But I care because of you, Cricket thought, watching him. *I might never have known any of this, if it wasn't for you.*

"I know plenty," Swordtail grumbled under his breath.

"I think Cricket is different from all the others," Sundew said. There was something in her voice . . . as though she needed to convince herself that was true.

"Maybe not. What do you think, Cricket? Are there any other HiveWings who are . . . who can't be . . . I mean, whose brains are like yours?" Blue asked Cricket, glancing around nervously.

"Not that I've ever met," Cricket said. "But we wouldn't exactly introduce ourselves that way, so how would I know?" She thought of that first day she'd seen everyone's eyes go white. "There was one dragon long ago; I think he was trying to fight it. But the queen used everyone in the Hive to catch him and bring him to her. I don't know what happened to him, but I'd guess he's not available for interviews."

Blue shivered, and she brushed his wing, trying to be as reassuring as she could be in public. The dragons around them were so loud and moving so quickly that she didn't think they'd notice anything beyond the bargains in their talons, but still. They had to be careful, for Blue's sake.

"Is that the Salvation Statue?" Swordtail whispered.

Cricket craned her neck up and spotted the head of the dragon that loomed over the center of the Glitterbazaar. It wasn't the real Queen Wasp, but the details of the stonework were so accurate that Cricket half expected the statue to suddenly twist around and glare at her.

But it didn't. The stone queen stayed frozen in place, wings flung out triumphantly, one talon holding up the Book of Clearsight.

Cricket stumbled, suddenly remembering the rest of the statue that commemorated the end of the war. The marble dragon that lay dead below the queen's other talons, with one of her deadly wrist stingers plunged through his heart. She'd never stopped for a moment to think about that dragon, because he wasn't anyone in particular. He was just "the enemy." He was a blank nobody representing the tribe who'd been defeated and exterminated when the HiveWings "saved" the SilkWings from them.

He was a LeafWing.

She glanced back at Sundew. "I should have warned you," she said quietly. "This could be upsetting."

"Don't worry, HiveWing," Sundew muttered, twitching her cape closer around her shoulders. "I'm at full rage all the time. It can't get worse."

"All the time?" Blue said wonderingly. "Really? Don't you get tired?"

"Yes," she growled. "And that makes me furious, too."

They stepped out of the crowd into the space around the statue. Like the Salvation Mosaic in Cicada Hive, this monument was also set apart from its surroundings. A tranquil circle of grass surrounded it, strangely peaceful in the chaotic bustle of the market. Cricket noticed that most of the shopping dragons carefully went around the circle to avoid treading on the grass, unless they were going up to admire the statue.

It was really extraordinary, twice the size of any actual dragons, and carved from stone quarried in the northwest mountains of Pantala. An enormous ruby glinted from each of the queen's eye sockets, and gold letters were inlaid on the cover of the marble Book of Clearsight.

But the real book doesn't look anything like that, Cricket thought, gazing up at the fake book. *It's not shiny or enormous; it doesn't have a title emblazoned on it. It's not what's on the outside of the Book that counts; it's what's on the inside, and that's the part Queen Wasp has been lying about to everyone.*

She glanced at the outline of the heavy pouch under Sundew's cloak. *We should make a copy of it, in case anything happens to it. But if anything did happen to it . . . who would believe us that the copy was real?*

Swordtail was circling the statue, frowning and fiddling anxiously with his jeweled mask.

"Well?" Sundew hissed as he returned to them.

"I don't know," he confessed. "I don't see a place to leave a message that wouldn't immediately be seen. What would you do?"

"Knock it over," she muttered. "Smash it to pieces with my bare talons. Throw the broken rock chunks at everyone in this Hive." But she stalked forward and studied the statue with sharp eyes.

"Are you all right?" Blue whispered to Cricket.

"Me?" she said, startled. "Sure. I don't know . . . this statue makes me feel so guilty now. And the Book is all wrong. I wish dragons could read the real version."

He nodded. "I've been thinking about Clearsight," he said softly. "She wouldn't want a war or this life for her descendants or for the other two tribes. But I don't know how we're going to help everyone. We're just four normal little dragons."

"I know," Cricket agreed. "Well, three normal little dragons and one vengeful warrior dragon with an arsenal of terrifying bugs."

Sundew had paused near one corner of the statue's base. She turned casually and met Cricket's eyes. Swordtail stepped toward her and she poked him backward, tipping her head to beckon Cricket to her. There were only two other dragons on the grass circle with them: a father with a small dragonet, who were sitting on the far side of the statue, sharing a lemon pastry and talking about the story of the Salvation.

"What is it?" Cricket whispered.

Sundew cut her gaze toward the very bottom of the stone slab, where the corner met the grass. A tiny shard of stone was missing, leaving a small gap between the base and the ground.

Something pale green was shoved into the gap.

Cricket realized that Sundew had angled herself to shield Cricket from view of anyone passing in the marketplace. She reached down and quickly tugged the something free.

It was a leaf, folded into a square. Unfolded, a message was revealed, inked across the veins on the inside.

Midnight. Library. 5.

Her heart thumping wildly, Cricket refolded the leaf and slid it back into place. She didn't know what the "5" meant, but the rest seemed pretty clear.

"I think we have a way to find the Chrysalis," she said to Sundew under her breath. "And I think I know where we can hide until then."

CHAPTER 8

Cricket's mother, Cadelle, lived about eight levels above the Glitterbazaar, in a neighborhood of little residential squares and parks that was respectable but not the wealthiest part of the Hive. It looked fancy enough to Cricket, but she'd heard her mother complain for hours about the classless neighbors, the long climb to her job at the university, and the shabby condition of the streets.

And one thing Cadelle hated in particular was the water tower that stood in the center of the square, directly across from her house. It was ghastly, it was covered in rust, there was nothing more hideous in the world, why couldn't she have been given a house on the sky-view side instead, why did she have to look at it every day, was this her punishment for the two little monsters she'd loosed on the world, couldn't the Hive do something to make it more attractive, why didn't anyone else care, if *she'd* been designing the Hive she'd have put all the water tanks *under* the street or at least on a level where no one important had to look at them.

But on their first visit to Jewel Hive, Katydid and Cricket had decided that it would make a perfect hiding spot.

"Maybe not perfect," Katydid had conceded, testing the rickety, rusty iron legs that held it up. "You'll probably get wet. Not sure how you'll explain that."

"I'll think of something, if I need to," Cricket said. She'd flown up to the top of the tower to make sure she could open the hatch by herself. She was four then, but she'd figured out the complicated latch after studying it for a moment. This was where SilkWing workers would climb in and out to clean the tank, and where they'd pour in the new water, gathered from sinkholes under the savanna or transported by air from Lake Scorpion.

This was the first thing they did wherever they went, Cricket and Katydid. Cricket was already used to doing it on her own, too. In every new place, she looked for somewhere to hide. She needed somewhere she could get to quickly and quietly, in case Queen Wasp suddenly brainwashed everyone with her orders (or as Katydid called them, "whole-Hive commands"). She needed to be ready to vanish at any moment.

She'd never had to use the water tower, though. Their two visits had been short, and there hadn't been any all-Hive mind-control moments while they were in Jewel Hive.

So she just had to hope that it was as good a hiding place as they'd thought it would be.

The streets around her mother's house were mostly deserted; it was still fairly early in the morning, so most dragons had either gone to work already, or, more likely, were still asleep after desperately trying to outlast everyone else at the parties and salons the night before. But the posters of Queen Wasp's face seemed to loom larger than ever, her eyes glaring down at them around every turn.

Worse yet, new posters had sprung up on several of the walls throughout the Hive:

WANTED — WANTED — WANTED

FOR CRIMES AGAINST THE TRIBE AND THE SACRED

MEMORY OF CLEARSIGHT

EXTREMELY DANGEROUS — APPROACH WITH CAUTION

REWARD FOR ANY INFORMATION OR IDENTIFICATION THAT

LEADS TO AN ARREST

And underneath all that, drawings of Blue, Swordtail, and Cricket.

But not Sundew, Cricket noticed. *Queen Wasp doesn't want to admit that a LeafWing got all the way inside her own Hive. Even though hundreds of dragons must have seen her as we escaped with the Book. But if the queen says it didn't happen, that's the new truth. Is there anyone who would dare to disagree with her?*

Her heart seized and jumped every time they passed another dragon near one of the posters, every time a HiveWing glanced at them, every time she caught a glimpse of her own face on a wall behind someone's wings.

What will happen to us if we get caught? What does Queen Wasp do with traitors? I've never heard of one in my lifetime — is that because there haven't been any, or because she made them disappear?

I wonder what happened to that dragon who tried to fight back against the mind control.

The only thing I know for sure: if we get caught, I'll never see Blue again. He'll be thrown back in the flamesilk cavern.

And the rest of us? Will we be executed publicly? Or vanish without a trace?

She'd always lived with a quiet fear at the back of her mind that one day she'd be found out and the queen would be furious. But this new fear was like termites in her skull, much more constant and present and squirming through all of her thoughts.

When they reached the square her mother lived on, they had to wait out of sight, around a corner, until a pair of SilkWings finished polishing the art around the water tower.

Dragonfly Square was named for a hero of the Tree Wars (as were many spots all around the Hives), and it was decorated with sculptures of dragonflies in her honor. They ranged from tiny mobiles, each dragonfly as long as one of Cricket's talons, to one the size of a dragon, perched on the side of the water tank. Their shiny metallic blues and greens gave the square the strange vibe of an electrocuted garden.

Sundew peered around the square as the two cleaners packed up their things and set off down a side street. "What's the plan here?" she hissed. "We're hiding in one of the houses?"

"No." Cricket pointed at the tower. "In there. There's a hatch at the very top, near the ceiling."

Swordtail wrinkled his snout. "Um, isn't that . . . full of water?"

"Not all the way," Cricket said. "There's a ledge and room to breathe at the top."

He still looked skeptical, but Sundew was already striding toward the tallest house. Staying in its shadow, she spread her wings, tossing back the cape, and soared up the wall. She was in the open for two heartbeats, hopping from the roof to the top of the tower, and then she was hidden by the curve of the tank.

Cricket followed her along the same path, with Blue and Swordtail behind her. They all landed as quietly as they could on the top of the tank, but the *thunk* of their talons on the metal still echoed enough to make Cricket wince.

There was the hatch, and as before, she was able to get it open quickly. She slipped inside first, reaching down with her tail to see how much space there was between the roof and the water level.

It was higher than last time, just covering the ledge that ran around the inside at the top. Cricket dropped onto the flat, latticed surface with a small splash and edged around to the other side, where she and Katydid had stabbed one of three peepholes. Through the hole in the metal, she could see straight down to her mother's house.

Is she still in there, or did she leave for work already?

Has she seen my face on the posters? Did she tell the queen I'm her daughter?

Is she disappointed in me? Or did this just prove everything she thought about me all along?

Cricket sighed. It was dark in the tank, and a little eerie with the vast expanse of water silent below them. But she could feel the brush of Blue's wings as he came and settled next to her, comforting her without saying a word.

Mother might be disappointed. But being different from the other HiveWings . . . I think that makes me lucky.

Sundew closed the hatch behind her and for a very long time, the four of them sat quietly, each thinking their own thoughts.

Sundew is dreaming of vengeance; Swordtail is worrying about Luna. Blue is imagining being them, or me, or any of the dragons who live in this Hive. I wonder if he would understand my mother. If he met her, could he explain her to me?

Cricket could just picture her mother's face if she ever brought Blue home for dinner.

She tried to focus on the mind control. Would the Chrysalis know anything she didn't? If they combined their research, would it reveal something new? Was it possible they were working on a way to free the HiveWings?

Or at least Katydid, she thought. *If I could free Katydid, I could stop worrying so much.*

"We're stuck in here until midnight?" Swordtail whispered.

"Yes," Cricket whispered back, clearing the fog from her glasses with one of the silk scarves around her neck.

"Whew." She felt the ledge vibrate as he shook his head. "It's going to be a long day."

Sometime later, Cricket discovered she had nodded off when Blue nudged her awake. She was disoriented by the darkness, so it took her a moment to access her natural sense of time. Almost midday. Her talons and tail were entwined with Blue's, and she pulled them back and adjusted her glasses, glad he couldn't see her expression.

"Cricket," he said softly. "Is that your mother?"

She leaned up to the hole where he was peering out. Sure enough, down below a dragon was coming out of her mother's house. A dragon the color of tangerines, with black patterns zigzagging along her spine and out to the edges of her wings.

"Yes," she said. "That's Cadelle." She hadn't seen her since the last rainy season. Katydid kept sending messages asking to visit and Cadelle always said no. Sometimes she said no in strongly worded letters about how annoying and useless they were.

Why do I still want her to love me? Cricket wondered.

"Want me to drop a mango on her?" Sundew offered.

"You have a MANGO?" Swordtail asked indignantly.

"No, you acorn. It's a *metaphorical* mango."

"I don't see how metaphorical mangoes are going to do us any good," Swordtail muttered.

Cadelle hurried off toward the ramps that led to the upper levels. She taught history at Jewel Hive University, which Cricket had heard her describe as "a job where I teach my replacements, because what else are they going to do with this information."

She moved as purposefully and quickly as she always did. She didn't slow down or glance sideways as she passed the Wanted posters of Cricket and her friends.

Has she even noticed it's me?

Maybe she doesn't care.

Cadelle strode out of sight down one of the avenues and Cricket sighed. Her mother was a question that seemed as though it would never have an answer.

She was about to lie down again when she spotted a flicker of movement from behind one of the other houses.

Cricket paused, squinting toward it. Was it a trick of the light? Or was that shadow bigger than it should be?

Something moved again, and this time she was sure it was a dragon's head peeking out, glancing furtively around, and then withdrawing, like a snail testing the open air with its antennae.

Another few long moments passed, and then two dragons carefully slipped out of the shadows. They both wore half capes with hoods, of pale silver embroidered with emerald threads, and they kept their heads down as they crossed the square toward Cadelle's house.

One turned to check up and down the streets as the other crouched and pulled Cadelle's spare key out from behind the loose tile where she kept it.

Cricket gasped.

It wasn't just that the silver-caped dragon knew where the key was. It was the way she moved, the flick of her tail as she walked, the tilt of her head as she unlocked the door.

The dragon sneaking into her mother's house right now was Cricket's sister, Katydid.

CHAPTER 9

"That's my sister!" Cricket whispered to Blue, keeping her eye pressed to the hole. "What is she doing here? Why is she sneaking in instead of letting our mother know she's here? And who is she with?"

The other dragon was a lot bigger than Katydid, but it was hard to see many details through the tiny spyhole and from such a height. The dragon's scales that Cricket could see were yellow, with black stripes on the wings, but that didn't narrow it down very much.

Katydid got the door open and turned back to look at her partner. The other dragon said something, and then they split up. Mystery dragon went to the corner of the avenue where Cadelle had gone, presumably to keep watch. Katydid slipped inside and closed the door behind her.

"I have to talk to her," Cricket said, standing up.

"What?" Swordtail cried. "That's a terrible idea! Sundew, tell her that's a terrible idea."

"She could turn into Queen Wasp at any moment," Sundew pointed out.

"Exactly," Swordtail agreed. "You heard the boss."

"But as long as she's herself, I know she's the one HiveWing I can trust," Cricket said. "And I need to make sure she's all right. I never said good-bye." Her breath caught in her throat and she had to struggle for the next words. "Or . . . explained or told her I was going or anything. And now she's *here*, right where I can talk to her. I just have to."

"Of course you should," Blue said. She could hear a thread of guilt in his voice. She knew he was thinking about how she had left her sister behind forever because she'd been helping him. He didn't have to feel bad about that; it had been her choice. But she didn't have time to reassure him — she had to hurry before Katydid slipped through her claws.

"I'll be back as soon as I can," she said, flying up to the hatch.

"*If* you can," Swordtail said glumly. "If she doesn't lose her mind and go all white-eyed and take you to the queen."

"Well," Cricket said, shooting Sundew a grin as a beam of light lit the LeafWing's concerned face. "Get some vicious caterpillars ready for me."

She hopped out onto the roof and as she pulled the hatch shut, she heard Sundew's voice saying, "They're CENTIPEDES; what is WRONG with you dragons?"

Cricket peeked over the edge at the dragon standing guard. Whoever it was did seem kind of familiar. But she couldn't risk them trying to stop her — or deciding to turn her in.

She spread her wings and floated quietly, quietly down to the highest balcony of her mother's house. The door here was also locked — Cadelle was very careful — but the balcony led to the least welcoming guest room of all time, where Katydid and Cricket had slept on their visits. The sisters had fiddled with the latch until it was just broken enough not to be noticed, so they could get in and out secretly if they needed to.

Cricket slid her claw under the latch and wiggled it up. The doors swung open toward her and she quickly hopped inside and pulled them shut again.

Across the room, Katydid whirled around, clutching a stack of papers to her chest. Her face made Cricket feel as if a thousand butterflies had just burst into the sky at once.

"Katydid!" Cricket leaped over the thin sleep pallets and threw her wings around her sister.

"No way," Katydid breathed. "Cricket? This can't be real." She took Cricket's shoulders and held her out to study her face. "By the Hives, it's really you. Are you all right?"

"I am," Cricket said. "I'm so sorry, Katydid. I know you must have been so worried. Are *you* all right? What are you doing here?"

"Your face is on posters in every Hive!" her sister cried. "They're saying you tried to steal the Book of Clearsight! And that you're running around with a pair of SilkWings! Cricket, you have to turn yourself in and tell them it's all lies. I'm sure if we explain —"

"But it's not all lies," Cricket interrupted her. "Katydid, we *did* steal the Book of Clearsight. The lie is everything Queen Wasp has ever said about it. Nothing she's told us is true."

Katydid sat down suddenly, as though her legs had turned to sand. "Oh, Cricket. Why?"

"I don't know, to keep power, maybe? To make sure no one ever questioned her?"

"No — *why* did you steal the Book? What were you thinking?"

Cricket was thrown. "That's not the important part, Katydid. I was trying to help someone. But didn't you hear what I said? It's all lies — everything Wasp said about the Tree Wars, about the SilkWings joining our tribe, all of it!"

"I'm sure she had her reasons!" Katydid said. "But you're in so much trouble now, Cricket! I don't know how to help. I don't know how to fix it!" She pulled Cricket into another hug and Cricket felt how cold her sister's scales were.

"You don't have to fix it," Cricket said, holding her tight. "I just came to tell you I'm all right — and to make sure you are, too. Who's that dragon outside? Why are you here instead of Cicada Hive?" She glanced around the small, bare room as Katydid leaned back. "And what are you doing in Mom's house?"

"I came to get these," Katydid said. She picked up the pile of papers she'd dropped, and Cricket realized it was drawings of her — drawings her sister had done on their last visit, of Cricket sleeping, laughing, rolling her eyes. Katydid was a good artist; they really looked like Cricket. Much more than the Wanted posters did.

"As far as we know, no one has told the queen who you are yet," Katydid said. "Maybe they haven't recognized you, or maybe they're afraid to admit they know you. I don't know why Mother hasn't, but I was worried that the queen would see these drawings through her eyes and realize she must know you."

"But if you take them," Cricket said, "then isn't it possible she'll see them through *your* eyes?"

"I'm going to destroy them," Katydid said with a sigh. "The queen has been mind-hopping all over the Hives, looking for clues about you. I'm afraid she must have figured out she can't get into your head."

"She has," Cricket said sadly. "I'm sorry, Katydid. I tried to be so careful. But she was inside the Librarian — did you know that? She's ALWAYS inside the Librarian. As soon as a dragon becomes the Librarian and joins the Temple of

Clearsight, Queen Wasp takes over and never lets her control her own body ever again. Can you imagine how horrible that would be?"

"But everyone wants to be the Librarian," Katydid pointed out. "It's such an important position."

"Only because everyone doesn't know about this!" Cricket cried. "If they knew it meant giving up your free will forever, would anyone sign up for that?"

"I think you're exaggerating a little," Katydid said. She started gathering all the drawings. "Let's talk about this somewhere safer."

Why isn't she listening to me? Cricket watched her sister for a moment, puzzled. These were huge, world-shifting facts. The truth about the Book, about Queen Wasp and the Librarian . . . why didn't Katydid want to know more? How could she brush that information aside so easily? If someone told Cricket she'd been lied to her whole life, she'd want to grab the truth and rub it into her eyeballs.

"I can't go with you, Katydid." Cricket took one of her sister's talons in hers. "It's too dangerous. You could be taken over by Wasp at any moment."

A fierce struggle crossed Katydid's face. "That's true . . . but maybe we should go to her and confess. I was wrong to help you hide it all these years. Perhaps she can do something to fix you and make you like the rest of us."

"No!" Cricket said. "I don't want that! I would never want that!"

"So what are you going to do?" Katydid said, exasperated. "Hide in a water tower forever?"

"I have friends," Cricket said. "We're looking for answers. I'm going to finally find out the truth about everything."

Katydid let out a short bark of a laugh. "That really is what you want, isn't it? The truth about everything — even if it makes your life a million times harder."

"Katydid, why are you really here?" Cricket asked. "I mean, in Jewel Hive. You didn't come all this way for a few drawings, did you? Why aren't you home with Father? If you're so sure the queen is right about everything, why haven't you told her about me yourself?"

Her sister stepped over to the balcony and peered out through the slats in the door. "Because I'd be in trouble, too," she said. "And Lady Scarab wouldn't let me."

"Lady Scarab!" Cricket clambered over the sleep pallets again and peeked out the window next to the balcony. She could see the dragon waiting by the corner, twitching her wings and tail impatiently. Holy mother of trees. That *was* Lady Scarab.

Cricket had met the grouchy, majestic old dragon a few times in her life, and it had always been very mysterious and alarming. The other dragonets at school whispered all sorts of rumors about her. They swore she was older than the Hives, maybe as old as the Book (which couldn't possibly be true, but it sounded dramatic). They said she had once been so powerful she could knock over a tree by breathing on it. They said she boiled SilkWings in their cocoons and ate them.

None of that was true, but Lady Scarab never bothered correcting the stories. She didn't seem to care what anyone thought of her, not even when two of Cricket's schoolmates saw her in the hall and screamed and flew out the nearest windows.

What *was* true was that she was Lady Jewel's mother and Queen Wasp's aunt. She lived all alone in a giant mansion in Cicada Hive, with no servants or anyone else. No one knew why she didn't live in the same Hive as her daughter, although she also owned a mansion in Jewel Hive, which she visited from time to time.

One day soon after Cricket's mother left, Lady Scarab had appeared suddenly on their doorstep. Their father, bowing and confused, let her in and tried to offer her tea in the parlor, but Lady Scarab had announced that she wished to see Katydid and Cricket. So they lined up for her inspection, and she studied them through her spectacles.

"You look healthy," she'd said to Cricket.

"Yes, ma'am," Cricket had answered, thinking, *Why are you here? Aren't you the dragon with the telescope? How old are you really? Do you ever eat little HiveWings? IS THAT WHY YOU'RE PLEASED THAT I LOOK HEALTHY?*

"Terrarium Academy?" Lady Scarab demanded. "Really?"

"Um," Cricket said nervously. "My school? I didn't choose it."

"I did," their father interjected. "It's very practical. A down-to-earth place."

"No pun intended," Lady Scarab said with a wintry smile, but Father just blinked in confusion. "Fine, but don't let them grow moss on your brain, dragonet."

"I — I won't," Cricket stammered, although she had no idea how to stop her teachers if they decided to do that, and could they really do that? Had anyone done that before? What did they do, put moss seeds in students' ears? Did it really work without any light in there? She'd only gotten rid of the ensuing nightmares later by doing a lot of research and figuring out that Lady Scarab must have been joking, because growing moss on a dragon's brain was quite scientifically impossible.

"I understand Cadelle has left the family," Lady Scarab went on, turning to Katydid. "Are you managing without her?"

"Yes, your ladyship," Katydid said. "Thank you for asking."

"Well, let me know if you need anything," the old HiveWing had said in a ferocious you'd-BETTER-tell-me-if-anything's-wrong! sort of way. "I'm not far and I'm not dead yet. Don't be a proud hungry fool. And that dragonet needs new glasses." She'd flicked a claw at Cricket, and the unsettling thing was, she'd been right. Cricket had needed stronger glasses, but she was still amazed that Lady Scarab had figured that out just by looking at her.

"Yes, your ladyship," Katydid said, bowing.

And then Lady Scarab had swept back out of their lives.

But here she was, standing guard while Katydid stole from her mother's house.

"Wait, *why*?" Cricket asked. "What does Lady Scarab care? Did you say she won't *let* you turn me in?"

"She came bursting into the house the day the Wanted posters went up," Katydid said. "She made me pack a bag and told Father not to tell Queen Wasp anything — about you, or me, or her taking me away. And then she brought me here, over the web bridges. I think she figures Lady Jewel can protect us from the queen, if necessary, but I'm afraid she's wrong about that."

She's definitely wrong. No one can protect anyone, as long as Queen Wasp can take over Lady Jewel or Scarab herself at any moment.

"I don't understand," Cricket said, trying to follow the threads. "Why would Lady Scarab have anything to do with us? We're just a pair of random HiveWings to her. Aren't we?" Katydid started rubbing her face with a miserable expression. "Katydid, what? What aren't you telling me?"

"Cricket, why do you always have to know everything?" Katydid cried. "Your life would be so much easier if you didn't. Wondering about SilkWings, asking impertinent questions about the queen's powers . . . and then stealing the Book of Clearsight! I was afraid you'd get in trouble one day, but I didn't think it would be this bad."

"But wouldn't you rather know the truth than live in a cloud of lies?" Cricket asked, confused. "I mean — wouldn't everyone?"

"No!" Katydid crushed the drawings between her claws. "Everything was fine! You were safe! No one ever needed to know about you, *especially* you."

Cricket felt her wings trembling, the way they sometimes did when she was close to an answer she'd been looking for.

"Katydid —"

"Cadelle is not your mother," Katydid blurted. "And Father is not your father, either."

Cricket stared at her. That . . . was not what she'd expected to hear. Although it explained a lot about the way they acted around her.

"But — then who —" she started.

A loud pounding came from the door downstairs, making them both jump. They peeked out the window and saw Lady Scarab thwacking it impatiently with her tail.

"She told me to be quick," Katydid said. "Cricket, come with us. I'll tell you everything, if I have to."

By the Hives, those were words Cricket lived for. Everything! Mysteries explained, puzzles solved! The whole truth, finally revealed to her!

But her friends were waiting in the water tower. They didn't know how to get to the library for the midnight meeting with the Chrysalis. They wouldn't understand if she left with Katydid. And it really wasn't safe — Queen Wasp could look out of her sister's eyes at any moment. Cricket had already stayed too long.

"I can't go with you," she said. "Can't you tell me everything now? Like, really quickly?"

Katydid hugged her fiercely. "It's not that easy. I just want you to be safe."

"I can only be safe if I know the truth," Cricket said, pulling back. "Just like our tribe will only be safe if they stop believing Wasp's lies."

Her sister sighed. "I don't see why. They're perfectly safe now, whatever you think she's lying to them about. Oh, Cricket, I have to go, but I'm afraid I'll never see you again."

"Can I find you?" Cricket asked. "Tomorrow. Around dawn?"

"I'll be hiding at Lady Scarab's house," Katydid said, pressing Cricket's front talons between hers. "Please be careful."

"You too." Cricket hugged her again and let go.

Katydid hurried out of the room with the drawings and Cricket heard her claws on the stairs. A few moments later, she came out the front door and locked it behind her, and then the two HiveWings flew away, with Lady Scarab scolding Katydid in a furious undertone.

Cricket stood in the barren room, looking at the empty walls and toyless shelves. She had cried herself to sleep in this room, wondering why Cadelle had taken Katydid to dinner and left her behind. She had cried in other rooms like this, wondering what was wrong with her, that her own mother didn't care about her. She had stared across the breakfast table at her blank-faced father, who never asked questions about school or her life unless she got in trouble — and then it was usually something like, "You still here? How long until you graduate? Quit bothering your teachers and stay out of my way."

A part of her had always thought everything would make sense once she knew why she was different — once she had the whole truth in her talons.

But this wasn't a truth she could get her talons around.

They weren't her parents. They never wanted her in the first place.

Someone gave me to them against their will.

So now the question was . . . who? And why?

PART TWO

A TRAIL OF SILK

— CHAPTER 10 —

Midnight. Library. 5.

Cricket tried all day to focus on what that "5" meant, but she couldn't keep her buzzing mind away from the mystery of her parents. She leaned over the ledge and trailed her claws through the cold, dark water. Beside her, Blue shivered as though he felt the chill traveling through her bones into his.

Cadelle is not your mother. Father is not your father.

Dragonfly Square was busy in the early evening as everyone bustled home from work to change into their nighttime glamour before going out again. Swordtail, watching through the spyhole, reported that Cadelle had sailed off with a very orange male dragon, but Cricket couldn't bring herself to watch.

Her whole life she'd been waiting for her mother to care about her. She didn't know how to dig up those seeds and replant them. She'd wanted something true she could put in front of her parents so she could say, "Look, here's why I'm different. Look, I found all the answers. Look, here's why you should love me anyway."

But they would never care. She wasn't theirs.

So whose was she? Where were her real parents?

It was also unsettling, as she thought over their conversation, to realize that nothing she'd said had made any difference to Katydid (*who is not actually my sister*, Cricket thought before her brain shied away from thinking about that). Cricket rubbed her forehead and tried to pull her scarves closer, but they didn't make her any warmer. She'd *tried* to tell Katydid about Wasp's lies, and Katydid had acted like the truth was just another story, another version of the world, instead of the only real version.

Wouldn't you rather know the truth?

No.

I think you're exaggerating.

I'm sure she had her reasons.

How could Katydid *say* that? Queen Wasp lied so that the HiveWings could take over Pantala, and she nearly wiped out the LeafWings to do it. She made them all think they were following Clearsight's plan. She convinced everyone she had the right to rule over the SilkWings — that the HiveWings were the strongest tribe, that they deserved everything they wanted. She turned her own dragons into murderers and monsters.

Maybe that's what Katydid didn't want to see.

Maybe I just need to try again. If I show her the Book . . . if she meets Blue and Sundew and takes a moment to understand them . . . if I tell her everything and try harder, she'll have to see. She'll have to hear me.

"Are you all right?" Blue whispered, taking one of her talons in his.

"Oh — sort of. Not really," she whispered back. "Cold. Also my whole life was a lie. But mostly cold." She nudged her glasses up and tried to smile at him.

"I can maybe help with that," he said. A softly glowing thread of flamesilk unfolded from his wrist, snaking out toward her scales. She started to pull away, but he held on to her gently. "Wait," he said. "I've been experimenting. This kind shouldn't burn you."

Cricket went still, realizing again how much she trusted him. The gold thread reached for her like a vine growing too fast; it wound around her claws and his and spiraled up toward her shoulder. Everywhere the flamesilk touched her scales, warmth sank in, quietly spreading into her bones.

"Oh, wow," she said softly. "It's like magic, Blue."

"Right?" he said. "I thought it would be much scarier. But I kind of love my flamesilk . . . is that weird?"

She shook her head. "I love it, too." She glanced over to the other side of the ledge, where Swordtail had accidentally fallen asleep on Sundew's cape. The LeafWing sat pinned beside his snoring head, glowering and tapping one of her pouches with an ominous look in her eyes.

"I miss my moms," Blue said softly.

"Oh," Cricket said. "I'm so sorry, Blue."

"As I was coming out of the cocoon," he said, "for a moment I forgot everything that had happened. I thought I would open my eyes and Mother and Silverspot would be there, waiting for me and smiling and ready to hug me and take me flying. I've been trying not to think about them too much . . . but, just for a moment, that felt so real. I hope they're all right. They must be worried about me and Luna, especially with all those posters up."

Cricket leaned into him. "Queen Wasp won't hurt them," she said. "It wouldn't accomplish anything, and she's very efficient. Maybe there's a way to get a message to them? Let's think. If we could find a SilkWing going to Cicada Hive . . ." She tried to think of SilkWings who traveled between the Hives — traders? Messengers?

"You've been really quiet all day," Blue said.

She sighed. "I know. It's . . . my sister told me that my parents aren't my parents."

In the glow from the flamesilk, she saw his eyes widen. "Wow." He thought about that for a moment. "So who are your real parents?"

"I don't know." And how was Lady Scarab connected? She

couldn't be Lady Scarab's daughter, could she? But then why wouldn't Scarab have kept her? That was too weird to even brush with her wings. Scarab had had *one* daughter, Lady Jewel, ages and ages ago. Cricket couldn't fit into her brain the possibility that Scarab had had another egg, decades later, with some mystery dragon and then given it away to Cadelle.

"Katydid didn't tell you anything else?" he asked.

She shook her head. "She really didn't want to. Blue, this has to be connected to why I'm different from the other HiveWings, doesn't it? Maybe one of my real parents is resistant to the mind control, too. Maybe Queen Wasp found out, and that's why they had to hide me with another family."

He was silent, and she tipped her snout toward him. "Blue?"

"I just can't imagine leaving my dragonet with someone else," he said. "That must have been so hard. There must have been a really big reason they couldn't keep you." His eyes met hers again and then dropped away quickly. "Like . . . if they weren't supposed to be together at all."

She gasped and covered her snout with her talons. Across the water tower, Sundew twisted to look at them.

It would never have entered her head before she met Blue. She wouldn't have been able to imagine it, until it changed her own life.

"You think one of my parents was a SilkWing?" she whispered.

"Do you?" he whispered back.

It's not possible. Is it?

Am I a hybrid?

Would hybrids be immune to the mind control? SilkWings are. Is that why I am?

It seems like such an obvious possible answer . . . why didn't I ever think of it before?

Because I thought I knew my parents.

Is that the answer?

But if that's the answer . . . how do we save the other HiveWings? We can't exactly turn them all into hybrids.

"I don't know." She tried to think of all the SilkWings she'd ever met. Had any of them acted strange, like maybe they were secretly her mother or father? Not that she could remember. There was no science on potential SilkWing-HiveWing hybrids. They were so forbidden it wasn't even conceivable to study the idea. Wouldn't there be something more . . . more *SilkWing* about her, if she were a hybrid?

Blue's antennae twitched. "It's almost midnight," he said.

"Thank the trees," Sundew responded. She yanked her cape out from under Swordtail, dumping him into the vat of water. When he came up sputtering and indignant, she flung her tail around his snout. "Shush, you great screech owl. It's time to go."

"It'll be all right," Blue said softly to Cricket, under the noise of Swordtail hauling himself out of the water. "I'm sure whatever happened, your real parents loved you and wished they could have kept you."

Cricket was not so sure, but she was relieved to be moving again, out of the tower and on their way to the library, a place that had always been full of answers for her. She hoped the Chrysalis SilkWings would be like that, too. Full of answers . . . if she could figure out what "5" meant and find them.

The library was a few levels up from Cadelle's neighborhood, just above the Jewel Hive Nest and below several levels of expensive ballrooms and wealthy mansions. It was one of Cricket's favorite places in all the Hives, and she always wondered why Jewel Hive was only famous for the Glitterbazaar. Why didn't other dragons ever talk about the library that took up an entire level, containing every book ever written by a HiveWing? Perhaps because it didn't fit with the image of Jewel Hive — no one imagined the dragons here choosing reading over shopping or jewelry-making.

And yet for some reason Lady Jewel wanted this library, Cricket thought as they crept up to the enormous double doors at the front entrance. *She made sure it was built into her Hive plans. None of the other Hives have one quite this big, not even Mantis Hive, which is supposed to be the smart Hive, the academic center of innovation.* Cricket looked up at the flying beetles carved over the doors. The joke in the other Hives was that Lady Jewel couldn't even read, although surely that wasn't really true. *Still . . . why did Jewel want a library that she apparently never goes into?*

Despite Jewel Hive's reputation, the library was never empty, at least as far as Cricket had seen. There were always dragonets everywhere — sprawled along the tops of bookshelves, curled in the window nooks, lying in the hammocks, and reading, reading, reading.

But now, near midnight, it was closed and deserted. The front doors faced the entrance from the ramps; there was a small plaza here, outside the library walls, with a circle of benches arranged around a statue of Clearsight.

Cricket loved this statue, too. Clearsight had her nose in a book — not The Book, just a book — and she was reading. She didn't look like an avenging prophet announcing the doom of all the tribes. She looked as though she might glance up any moment, see Cricket, and say, "Oh my gosh, have you read this one? It's amazing!"

The entire library level was vibrating from the shouts and music of a party above them. The flamesilk globes overhead shook and swayed and sent shadows wobbling across the front of the library. Tiny flecks of treestuff drifted down, making Cricket sneeze.

"Where's the Chrysalis?" Sundew whispered to Swordtail.

He spread his wings in a "how would I know?" gesture, and she rolled her eyes.

"You're not the most useful revolutionary," she hissed. "Has anyone ever told you that?"

"I'm better with Luna around," he said wistfully.

Sundew hopped up the library steps and tried the doors, but they were locked. "So if we can't get in," she said, turning with a swirl of her cape, "the meeting must be out here in the plaza, right?"

Cricket looked around. It felt as if they were completely alone on this level. They'd passed other dragons on the ramps up and down, but it was the glittering hours of the night: all of them were going past the library to the gatherings above, to glitter and see and be seen glittering.

"Have you ever noticed that glitter is a word that quickly loses its meaning if you say it too much?" she said to Blue. "Glitter. Glitter. Glittering. Isn't it super weird now?"

"You're super weird," he said affectionately. "Why isn't this library as sparkly as the rest of the Hive?"

She glanced up at the towering walls of treestuff. It was true; unlike most of Jewel Hive, the library wasn't shimmering with embedded jewels and tiles and decorations. It did have expensive wooden doors, saved from some long-ago building that must also have been a library, because they had books carved all over them.

Cricket remembered Sundew slashing her claws through the sculpted face of Queen Wasp on the doors of Wasp Hive. She wondered how long it had taken to carve the doors there and here, and whether there was any way to repair the damage, and who still knew the skills of wood carving and what kinds of tools were required . . .

Blue climbed the steps and touched the wooden door lightly with his talons. She saw a sad look cross his face as he glanced over at Sundew.

He's thinking about what she might be feeling, Cricket guessed. *That thing he does, where he's always in someone else's head.* She thought it was fascinating; she wished she could remember to do it like he did.

I could try now . . . he's thinking . . . hmmmm. Maybe that seeing wood used for doors must make Sundew sad . . . because she misses the trees?

"Any ideas?" Sundew barked, poking Cricket's shoulder. "You three look half asleep. Do I need to bring up Belladonna's other plan and our time limit? You do *want* to find the Chrysalis, don't you?"

Cricket shivered at the reminder. The Chrysalis *had* to

have answers for them, if they wanted to stop Belladonna and the other LeafWings.

"It doesn't seem like they're coming," Swordtail said. He peered off along the walls in either direction.

"We're missing something," Cricket said. "Five. That was the third part of the message. Five . . . doors of the library? But there are only these, from the ramps, and another set at the back that open out to the savanna. Those will be closed at night, too." She scanned the plaza. "There are only four benches. Nothing with a five on it, right?"

Blue squinted at the doors. "I don't see any fives up here."

"Maybe the statue . . . like where the message was hidden in the Glitterbazaar?" Cricket walked around the statue of Clearsight, looking for tiny cracks where another leaf might be stuffed. Nothing in the base. Nothing under Clearsight's talons. Her neck curved toward the book, the row of spines spiraling along her back down her tail.

The spines were the only thing Cricket could see where there were more than five of them. She hopped up onto the statue's base and reached up to the top of Clearsight's head. One, two, three, four, five spines down her back — and there was something lodged under the fifth one.

A key.

She tugged it out and studied it in the light of the flickering flamesilk globes.

"What is it?" Sundew asked, resting her front talons on the base of the statue and lifting her neck to see.

"Our way into the library, I think," Cricket said.

Sure enough, the key fit the lock on the doors. Swordtail heaved one side open and they slipped inside, one by one, while Cricket returned the key to its hiding spot and then followed them. Inside, there was a bolt to lock the doors again behind them.

A kind of peace settled over Cricket as she stepped into the library. She always felt this way when she was surrounded by books. She belonged here, even if she didn't fit anywhere else. In here there were answers and information and thousands of stories waiting for her to fold herself into them. She was always safe inside a book.

And this was her favorite of all the libraries she knew. Shelves radiated out from the central desk in every direction, like a sunburst, and more aisles with more books filled the balconies overhead. Beloved characters were painted on the walls, golden glass and copper wire dragons holding books hung from the ceiling far overhead, and blue silk tapestries filled the rest of the open space, woven with quotes about reading.

"Hm," Sundew said quietly, glancing around. "There's a lot of dead trees in here."

Cricket was startled out of her peace. "They're not — I mean, maybe — but they're books! Books are everything!"

"And they're not all made from trees, right?" Blue offered.

"Right." Cricket shook out her wings, taking a calming breath. "We mostly make paper from silk now."

"Oh, good," Sundew answered. "You used up our resources and moved on to exploiting a different tribe."

"But the books are for us, too," Blue said. "For everyone. I'd give all my silk to help build a place like this." He ducked his head and looked at Cricket, and she wished she could throw her wings around him and tell him how wonderful he was.

Sundew wasn't wrong. She kept opening Cricket's eyes in moments when Cricket hadn't realized they were closed. But Blue was the reason she could keep them open and still feel all the things she felt. He saw Cricket; he understood completely what this place meant to her.

"Shh," Sundew said, flicking her tail in front of Swordtail's face even though he hadn't said anything at all. She pointed up and gave Cricket a quizzical look.

She could hear it, too. Voices arguing, somewhere upstairs.

They could have flown up to the balcony that overlooked the first floor, but their wingbeats might have scared away the other dragons. *If they can hear anything over their own voices, that is,* Cricket thought as they crept up the stairs instead.

This was certainly the loudest stealth meeting of a secret rebellion she'd ever heard.

"No, *you're* doing it wrong!" one of them shouted. "It's like *you* don't even care about what we're trying to do here!"

"I'm focusing on what's actually important!" another one yelled back. "Tearing apart other SilkWings isn't going to get us anywhere!"

"We have to fix the problems in our own tribe before we can stand together," the first voice insisted. "I mean, if I think Argus is a lazy caterpillar who doesn't understand our mission, then it's *useful* for me to yell at him until he sorts himself out."

"I think it's cowardly," the second voice snapped back. "It's easy to yell at Argus because he's on our side. It's a lot easier than standing up to the dragons we're *supposed* to be fighting."

"I'm sure your intentions are good, Morpho," pleaded a third voice as Cricket and her friends crept through the stacks. "But what if you've scared him away and he never comes back?"

"Then good riddance," the first voice snapped.

"No!" shouted the second. "We need every dragon we can get on our side! I'd rather have fifty SilkWings who are at least *trying* to do the right thing than three who are perfect in every way by *your* standards."

Sundew crouched and snuck a glance around the last corner. Through the bookshelves, Cricket could see bright blue wings flashing open and closed, and the pale yellow scales of another dragon close by. They were in the back corner of the library, farthest from the front doors, near a wall of windows that looked out onto the dark savanna. Cricket remembered this reading nook with its hammocks and pillows. The flamesilk lamps were covered for the night, but their light still glowed dimly through the dark silk shades, illuminating the books scattered on the windowsills and the floor.

They should be more careful, Cricket thought nervously. Dragons flew between the levels all night in Jewel Hive, flitting from one party to another. Someone could easily fly past the library windows, glance inside, and wonder why a group of SilkWings was in the library after dark.

"You go out there first," Sundew whispered to Swordtail. "Make sure they don't freak out when they see the rest of us."

"Me?" Swordtail said. "I mean, right. Me. Introductions. No freaking out. No problem." He squared his shoulders and took a deep breath. "What should I say?"

"Just figure it out," Sundew hissed.

"You'll be great," Blue added reassuringly as Sundew shoved Swordtail toward the squabbling dragons.

"Right," Swordtail said. He cleared his throat and

stepped between the hammocks, into the dim circle of light. "Excuse me? Hi."

The SilkWings whirled around and stared at him.

"I'm looking for the Chrysalis," said Swordtail.

One of the dragons snorted and spread his wings at the other two SilkWings with him. "Well, congratulations," he said. "You've found us."

—— CHAPTER 11 ——

"Oh — good," Swordtail said. "Great. Um. Hello, Chrysalis."

"What kind of secret organization just admits who they are to any idiot who walks in?" Sundew muttered. She flicked her tail, swiping Cricket with the billow of her cape. "They have no idea who he is or who he's with!"

Cricket crouched to get a clearer view through the shelves, but she could still only see three dragons in the reading nook. Was that it? The whole Jewel Hive faction of the secret SilkWing rebellion was . . . three arguing dragons?

"Why were you looking for us?" demanded the dragon with bright blue wings. He was the owner of the first voice — Morpho, if Cricket remembered right. His torso was dappled with iridescent sea-green scales and little patches of white ran down his tail, but he had clearly been named for the color of his wings, which were nearly as vibrant as Blue's.

"Maybe he wants to join us," said the pale yellow dragon hopefully. "Do you dream of a better world, friend?"

"Do you agree that all SilkWings should refuse to serve any HiveWings in the Glitterbazaar?" the blue dragon demanded. "And that we should make lists of all the Silk-Wings who do so we can go yell at them?"

"Oh, *honestly*, Morpho," said the third dragon, rolling her eyes.

Swordtail cleared his throat nervously. "Um . . . my name is Swordtail. I'm part of the Cicada Hive Chrysalis — I mean, sort of — I was about to be. Me and Luna. And now she's missing. Have you heard anything about a dragon named Luna recently? Has she come to you for help, maybe?"

The three dragons blinked at him in confusion.

"I don't know anyone named Luna," said the yellow dragon. "I'm sorry," she added as Swordtail's wings drooped.

"She's a flamesilk," he said. "We rescued her, but she might have been recaptured by Wasp Hive. Have you heard anything like that? A SilkWing taken prisoner over Dragonfly Bay in the last five days?"

They all shook their heads, and Swordtail's wings drooped even more. "Are you sure?" he asked. "Maybe she's hiding with another wing of the Chrysalis?"

"Maybe," the yellow dragon said gently. "We haven't heard anything."

Cricket reached over and squeezed one of Blue's talons.

He looked so worried and sad . . . she wished she had a tiny fraction of Clearsight's power so she could have a vision of Luna and let Blue know his sister was all right.

"Is that why you're here?" asked Morpho. "Just looking for another SilkWing?"

"Not just that. My friends and I were hoping you could help us," Swordtail said.

Morpho squinted at the shelves behind Swordtail, while the other two dragons exchanged a worried glance. "Your friends? Who's with you?"

Swordtail turned and beckoned. Sundew rolled her eyes at Cricket. "Very thorough introduction, Swordtail," she whispered. "This is going to go great."

Blue stepped out first, sliding up beside Swordtail. Before he could speak, the yellow SilkWing jumped forward with a gasp.

"You're the one from the Wanted posters!" Her pale yellow antennae unfurled all the way and she stared at him as if he were a tree who'd just sprouted illegally in the middle of the library floor.

"Hey, I was on the posters, too," Swordtail pointed out.

"Are you really a flamesilk?" the third dragon asked, reaching toward Blue's talons and then catching herself and pulling back.

"Yes," he said, turning his wrists upward so she could see the embers glowing under his scales.

"Oh, wow," she said. "That was the rumor but no one will officially confirm it. How did you escape?"

"And wasn't there a HiveWing on that poster with you?" Morpho asked suspiciously.

"That's how," Blue said to the dark orange dragon who was studying his wrists. "And that's why she's wanted by the queen, too. She helped me escape." He turned and held out one talon toward Cricket. "Cricket?"

Cricket took a deep breath and stepped out to stand beside him. Morpho leaped back and hissed in alarm. The other two seized blankets off the floor and threw them over their heads with high-pitched yelps of terror.

"It's too late!" Morpho snapped at them. "She's already seen your faces. I told you this was a stupid meeting place!"

"No, you didn't!" cried the small dark orange dragon from under her blanket. "You suggested it!"

"Cinnabar's right," agreed the muffled voice of the yellow dragon.

"It's not important who's right!" Morpho shouted. "Although it was me! But what's important is that there's a HiveWing right here and what are we going to do about it and also it was your fault we couldn't meet at my better suggestions, so there!"

The yellow dragon winced, and Cricket noticed that one of her back wings, sticking out from under the blanket at an awkward angle, was smaller than all the others. She wondered if the SilkWing could fly at all.

"Wait, wait," Cricket said as the yellow dragon started edging toward the nearest aisle with the blanket still over her head. "You don't have to hide! I'm a friend, I promise."

"Friends don't let their brains get invaded and betray the revolution," said Cinnabar, pulling her wings and tail under her blanket and huddling into a small boulder as if she hoped everyone would forget she'd been there.

"That won't happen," Cricket said. "The mind control doesn't work on me."

The SilkWings fell silent for a moment, even Morpho, with his mouth half open. Then the yellow dragon threw her blanket off and stared at Cricket. Her wings — well, three of them — were long and narrow and her scales were a mix of pale yellow and pale brown, like bananas and cashews mashed together. She had dark amber eyes and gold stripes painted on her claws.

"What are you talking about?" she asked.

"Nope. Not possible," Morpho declared. "HiveWing LIE."

"But it is possible, because there's me," Cricket said. "I know, it's weird and I can't explain it. The queen can't get into my head, I promise you. I wish I knew why! I've been trying to figure it out my whole life."

And the closest I've gotten is the theory that I'm half SilkWing. But nothing about me is very SilkWing — I mean, I think I look like a HiveWing from horns to claw tips. I don't have a natural weapon, but neither do a lot of HiveWings. I know I'm different somehow . . . but I still feel like a HiveWing.

She decided not to mention the SilkWing theory yet. She needed more evidence first.

"This seems like a trick," Morpho muttered. He stalked toward her and peered into her eyes. His were the same emerald green as his antennae, which curled and waved as though he was trying to sense the presence of Queen Wasp inside her.

"It could be true," said the yellow dragon. "She could be like the ones we heard about."

Cricket felt her heart speed up. "Other dragons like me? Who?"

"We don't know for sure. Cinnabar, come out and tell her about the story you heard."

The blanket boulder sighed enormously, and then the small orange SilkWing poked her head out. "If you're going to keep using my name in front of total strangers, you could at least introduce yourself, too, Tau."

"Oh, sorry," said the yellow dragon gently. "I'm Tau, that's Cinnabar, and that's Morpho."

"And I never said I believed that story," Cinnabar pointed out. Her scales were a burnt orange with glints of dark red under her wings and along her spine. With a few black scales, slightly different wings, and a much scarier expression, she could almost have passed for a HiveWing.

"What story?" Cricket asked.

Cinnabar flicked the blanket off with her wings and edged closer to Tau. "It's just a rumor. I heard it from a SilkWing who heard it from his cousin who heard it from a traveling theater performer. The whisper is that there's a home for old dragons in Tsetse Hive, where none of them are allowed to leave ever because the queen can't mind-control them."

"Fairy-tale nonsense," Morpho spat. "She controls everyone."

"No, Morpho, you know that's not true," Tau said. "She doesn't Hive-mind her sisters, or Lady Jewel."

"She doesn't?" Cricket tilted her head. She'd never heard that before.

"But she *could*, if she wanted to," Morpho insisted. "She just doesn't because she likes to give them the illusion of control. As long as they think they have their own Hives to run, they'll bow and scrape and let her be the one who's really in charge of everything."

"You've said that before," Tau said, a tiny sliver of impatience slipping through her peaceful mask. "But I am sure it doesn't work on Lady Jewel. I've been with her when the whole Hive is taken over, like when the entire tribe was sent to find these two." She gestured at Blue and Cricket.

"Three!" Swordtail protested, finally looking up from his talons. "They're hunting for me, too!"

"She finds it *very* irritating," Tau went on. "Her whole day is disrupted and all Jewel Hive business has to be put on hold and she has to sit for hours waiting for her subjects to come back. She can't even hide how annoyed she is from the SilkWings who work for her."

"That's true," Cinnabar agreed. "Even in the kitchen we can tell; it's nonstop sugar orders all day."

"That doesn't prove anything," Morpho argued. "Wasp probably enjoys knowing how annoyed Jewel is. I don't believe there's a single HiveWing she can't control if she wants to."

"Listen," Cricket said reasonably. "If Queen Wasp could control me, would I be on a Wanted poster? Wouldn't she just march me into her Hive from inside my brain? And use me to catch these two?"

Morpho opened and closed his mouth a few times.

"Oh, wow," Cinnabar said. "You actually shut Morpho up for a moment. You can definitely be in *my* Chrysalis."

"This is a trap!" Morpho exploded. "HiveWings can't be trusted! None of them!"

"You're just mad because this proves what Tau and I have been saying," Cinnabar snapped back. "We *could* get HiveWings on our side if they were allowed to think for themselves!"

"I don't know about that," Swordtail said. "Cricket might be the only one."

Cricket's scarves felt too tight around her neck. He had to be wrong. The other HiveWings couldn't be lost forever. She just had to find a way to set them free.

"I think you're right," she said to Cinnabar. "I mean, I hope so. Do you know anything else about Queen Wasp's mind control? Like, how it works, or whether anyone's ever managed to break free from it?"

Tau blinked and shook her head sadly. "Oh, I see," she said. "You're trying to free someone, too. I'm sorry; I've never heard of anyone escaping the mind control."

"And even if they did," Morpho growled, "all the HiveWings have had Queen Wasp in their heads for so long, they can't think for themselves anyway. They'll keep believing her lies, no matter how free you think they are."

Cricket shivered, remembering her conversation with

Katydid. *I will get through to her. If I keep telling her the truth, she'll have to hear me — she'll have to believe me.*

Something flashed outside the window, like silver catching the moonlight, but when Cricket turned to look, it was gone. The night beyond the glass was empty; only savanna grasses waved in the midnight breeze.

"I am not interested in wasting time on HiveWings," Morpho said firmly. "I want to save *SilkWings*. There are enough of us to win if we join together and rise up!"

Tau was shaking her head. "There aren't," she said. "It's too dangerous. Too many SilkWings would die. I'm sorry, Morpho, but we have no weapons, and they have the queen's Hive mind."

"Also stingers," said Swordtail helpfully. "And venom. And toxic paralysis stabber bits."

"Sounds like you need an army," Sundew said, timing her dramatic entrance perfectly. She emerged from behind the bookshelves and threw off her cape. Her leaf-shaped wings gleamed gold and green in the lamplight.

The Chrysalis SilkWings all gasped. Tau sat back and pressed her front talons to her heart. Cinnabar crouched as though she didn't know whether to fly or fight or scream. Morpho's eyeballs looked like they were full of sunbeams.

"Luckily for you," said Sundew, "we've got one."

"Wait, but you're not going to use it," Blue interjected. "Right, Sundew? That's why we're here, because we're looking for a better solution. We're going to find an answer for your parents so they don't restart the Tree Wars."

"You heard these dragons — there isn't one," she said, tossing her head. "There's no way to break the Hive mind. So, backup plan. I'm here to make contact with the Chrysalis. If the SilkWings are ready to join the LeafWings this time, maybe the new Tree Wars will turn out the *right* way."

"But, Sundew —" Cricket started, horrified.

The LeafWing brushed past her and held out one talon to Cinnabar. "What do you say? Care to destroy the HiveWings together?"

CHAPTER 12

"Sundew!" Blue cried.

Cricket felt as though the floor was turning to glue, trapping her claws in place. Sundew couldn't give up so quickly. There had to be something, some answer they just hadn't found yet. *Some way to save my tribe — to save all our tribes — from a new war.*

"YES," Morpho shouted, elbowing Cinnabar out of the way. He took Sundew's talon between his and pumped it up and down. "We're in!"

"You don't speak for the whole Chrysalis," Tau said to him. Cricket realized there were tears in her eyes as she stepped toward Sundew. "You're *alive*," she whispered. "I thought you were all dead. I thought we'd lost your whole tribe forever."

Sundew looked taken aback. "We had no idea any of you cowards cared," she said, a little awkwardly. "And no, we're not all dead."

I cared, Cricket thought. *I was so thrilled to find real actual alive LeafWings hiding in Queen Wasp's greenhouse. Didn't she see that I cared?*

"Sundew, what about freeing the HiveWings?" she said. "We wanted to give them a chance to make the right choice, remember? We agreed that breaking the mind control would help everyone."

Sundew shrugged, cascades of reflected gold glittering along her wings. "Like I suspected all along, it can't be done. The only option is to crush the HiveWings completely."

"YES," Morpho shouted again.

"Fine by me," said Swordtail. "I'm with Sundew."

Blue took a step closer to Cricket so he could brush her wings with his. "This isn't right," he said. "There are good HiveWings, I'm sure of it. I don't think we can solve a tragedy of the past by just repeating it in reverse."

"Well, *I* don't think we can solve a *current* tragedy by sitting around trying to understand the bad guys," Sundew snapped. "I don't want to hug a bunch of HiveWings and listen to their problems! I want them all punished!"

Cricket buried her face in her talons. *I would feel the same way in her place, wouldn't I?* But these were still her dragons. She couldn't give up on her entire tribe — on Katydid and Lady Scarab and the Librarian and the little dragonets on her street and her father (even if he wasn't her real father) and the students who'd shared books and seeds with her at school. She had to believe they were better than what Queen Wasp had turned them into, and that they could still be saved.

"Where do we start?" Morpho asked. "What do we have to do?"

Cinnabar glanced at Tau. "Wait. Not all of us want to kill all the HiveWings," she said.

"Or *any* HiveWings," Blue interjected.

"How many SilkWings are in the Chrysalis?" Sundew asked, ignoring them. "Tell me there are more than three of you."

"Oh, yes," said Morpho. "In this Hive there are *seven* of us."

Sundew did not look impressed. "Seven."

"Yes," he said. "Well. Maybe six."

"If you scared Argus away forever," Cinnabar added.

"Why aren't the others here?" Sundew flicked her gaze over the three of them and frowned slightly.

"They couldn't make it tonight," Tau said. "One had to make costumes for her dragonet's school play. Another has an early morning meeting. And what did Temora say?" she asked Cinnabar.

"That she was too tired," Morpho answered disapprovingly.

"Really," Sundew said. "Very dedicated to this rebellion, are they?"

"To be fair," Cinnabar said, "we haven't exactly *done* much at the last few meetings. Or ever. Actually ever. I mean, how can seven dragons change anything? We know there are more SilkWings in other Hives who want to fight back, too. But it's just . . . everyone's busy with their lives and no one knows what to do and, I don't know, it's overwhelming."

"But now that you're here," Morpho said to Sundew, "it's very clear, right? Bring in your army, violence everywhere, SilkWings help you, things get better."

"How?" Sundew asked. "How, exactly, do the SilkWings help us?"

Morpho shifted his wings with a confused expression. "By . . . doing whatever you want us to do? Maybe pointing to the worst HiveWings? Cheering when you kill them?"

Sundew sighed and rubbed her forehead.

There was another flash outside the window. Again, Cricket only saw it out of the corner of her eye, and when she turned, nothing was there. Maybe it was distant lightning. She pulled her scarves closer and stepped up to the dark glass.

For a moment, all she saw was her reflection and the reflections of the dragons behind her. For a moment, she was inside a glass box with strangers, the piece that didn't fit.

And then her eyes adjusted, just in time to see a pair of dragons swoop by right below the level of the window.

A pair of HiveWings, wearing armor and carrying weapons. And heading around the curve of the Hive, toward the back door of the library.

She whirled around. "I think we've been seen."

"Unlikely. No one pays attention to the library," Morpho argued.

"Shhhh," Sundew commanded, raising one claw.

They all fell silent.

A soft rattling sound came from the front door of the library . . . as though someone was trying a series of keys in the lock.

Cinnabar and Tau exchanged wide-eyed looks.

"They're at the back, too," Cricket whispered.

"Do we fight our way out?" Swordtail asked Sundew.

"We don't know how many there are," Cinnabar said. "And if any of them have Queen Wasp in them, she can summon a whole lot more in a heartbeat."

"Can you do that?" Morpho asked Sundew. "Summon a whole bunch of ferocious LeafWings?"

"Not with my mind," she said crossly. "Is there any other way out of the library?"

Tau shook her head. "Maybe if a couple of us attack them, the others can escape," she suggested.

"I don't want to leave anyone in the claws of the HiveWings," Blue said quietly.

Sundew whirled toward Cricket. "Your hiding place. You must have one nearby. Show us where you'd go if Wasp Hive-minded everyone while you're in here."

Cricket hesitated. She didn't know if all seven of them would fit. She also felt like there should be some conversation about betrayal and broken promises here, but there wasn't exactly time.

"This way." She hurried through the aisles with all of them rustling behind her. At the edge of the balcony, she vaulted over without stopping and sailed down to the first floor.

When she looked back, she saw Cinnabar throw Tau's weak pair of wings over one of her shoulders so she could support the yellow dragon down to the next level. As soon as they landed, Tau's wings folded back in and she was running again.

On either side of the front doors and on either side of the back doors stood a tall column, built into the wall and stretching from floor to ceiling. This was the book drop, with slots on the outer walls where dragons could slide in their returned books.

On the inner walls, each column had a door half as tall as a dragon, which the librarians could open to pull out the returned books. Cricket tugged one open and pointed inside.

"Got it," Cinnabar whispered. "Come on, Tau." The two of them ran off toward the back doors, to hide in one of the columns there.

"I'm going with the LeafWing," Morpho declared. He ducked in through the door Cricket was holding open, scrunching himself around the pile of books inside, and held out one talon toward Sundew.

"I can see how I deserve that," Sundew said, "but no, you get Swordtail." She bundled Swordtail into the cramped space with Morpho and closed the door on their protesting faces.

"Don't you want to be with your new Chrysalis friends?" Cricket couldn't help asking.

Sundew hurried across to the other column just as they all heard a *click* from the front door. Cricket's heart tried to hurl itself out of her chest. She scrambled inside the book drop, burrowing through and up the pile of teetering library books inside. A moment later, Blue squeezed in beside her, and then the space went dark as Sundew leaped inside and shut the door behind her.

Cricket braced herself against the walls and edged upward a little, but her wings were tangled with Blue's and their scales were pressed so close together that she could feel his heart beating all the way through her own chest. He rested one talon on the wall behind her, his cape drifting around them like extra silken wings. She tucked her head under his chin, breathing in the scent of old books and Blue, who smelled a bit like fried bananas.

Below them, she could sense the poised, still form of Sundew, still half-buried in books. The slide for the books from the upper slot ended near Cricket's head, and the edge dug into her neck, but she didn't dare try to move away from it.

I hope everyone else can be quiet, she thought anxiously. If the soldiers found dragons in one book drop, they'd check the rest and find all of them. *This wasn't the smartest hiding place. We should have spread out more.*

"Finally," said a voice outside the book drop. Blue tensed, sending little shivers through Cricket's scales. "Sorry that took so long. Lady Jewel has a lot of keys."

"And I suppose half of them are entirely decorative," sneered another voice — unfamiliar but also unmistakably in the thrall of Queen Wasp. Cricket had heard that sinister cadence so many times in situations just like this, hiding in the dark while the queen used her subjects as puppets.

Not just like this. She felt Blue's shoulder, cool and smooth against her neck. *This time I'm not alone.*

"Open the back doors for the others and then search every corner," the queen ordered through the HiveWing's mouth. Cricket heard two sets of talons walking away. She wondered why the queen wasn't inside them, too, or if she was now. *She might have needed one of them inside his own brain to get the library doors open*, she guessed. The HiveWing would supposedly have a better idea of which key would work than the queen would.

It still took a while, though, she thought gratefully. *Was that on purpose? Did that HiveWing help us by taking longer than he needed to?*

Perhaps that was wishful thinking.

He didn't know who was in here, if anyone . . . maybe he just wanted to annoy the queen.

Whatever his reasons, or even if he'd done it by accident, she was thankful.

A long time seemed to pass. They heard talonsteps and thumps, as though boxes were being overturned somewhere.

"No sign of anyone, Your Majesty," a voice reported after a long while.

"I know I saw dragons in here," the HiveWing with the queen inside hissed. **"Find them, or you will die."**

Blue flinched, and Cricket tensed for a moment, wondering if she'd accidentally scratched him.

But then she realized, *Oh, he's worried about the HiveWings out there, and what Queen Wasp will do to them if they don't find us.*

She didn't dare risk whispering, but she wished she could tell him that she'd never seen the queen force a dragon to hurt himself while she was controlling him. As they'd seen in the Temple of Clearsight, Wasp felt the same pain as the dragons she was controlling, and she would jump out of their minds if the pain was too much.

But she could still force a dragon to hurt someone else. There was nothing they could do, though, except turn themselves in, and Cricket wasn't going to let Blue do that. She was pretty sure Sundew wouldn't let him, either.

"Come out, you sniveling cowards!" Wasp's voice roared suddenly. "I know there are dragons hiding in this library! Show yourselves, or I will burn all the books until you die choking on the smoke."

Burn the books! She can't — she wouldn't. Jewel wouldn't let her. Could she stop the queen, though? Wouldn't burning the books put the rest of the Hive in danger, too? Maybe Wasp doesn't care about that. Maybe she'd burn down the whole Hive to smoke us out.

Cricket heard a soft hiss from Sundew below her.

Sundew couldn't give herself up — she was the one holding the Book of Clearsight, and they needed that to prove Queen Wasp was lying. She wouldn't let Blue go, either, as long as his flamesilk was part of the LeafWing plan.

But Cricket — she wasn't any use to the LeafWings, really. What would happen to her if she turned herself in to the queen?

Would she kill me?

Her wings were trembling and she couldn't make them stop.

I'm not brave. I'm not a warrior. I don't want to put myself in Queen Wasp's talons, not even to save all the books.

But if I don't, what happens to Blue and Sundew?

As if he could hear her thoughts, Blue curled himself closer to her and held her tightly, absorbing her trembling in his own wings.

"**Very well,**" said the queen's voice. "**Build me a bonfire of books right here,**" she ordered. "**We'll use flamesilk from the lanterns.**"

"But — Your Majesty — what if the fire spreads?" asked one of the HiveWings.

"**Then we'll have to throw you into it to slow the flames,**" the queen snarled. "**You are a tedious talonwringer. I'll do it myself.**"

Cricket heard the dragons snap suddenly to attention and run off toward the stacks without any further argument. She guessed that Queen Wasp had taken them over as well.

"Wait!"

Below her, Cricket heard a book slide down the pile; Sundew caught it deftly before it could *thunk* against the side. They all held their breaths, frozen in place, caught by the sound of Cinnabar's voice in the library.

"We're sorry. We're sorry, my queen."

"Very sorry." That was Tau.

What are they doing?

"We were hiding from Lady Jewel," Cinnabar said breathlessly. "She said we were spending too much time reading and not enough time on our work for her."

"So we've been sneaking out at night to read here," Tau said. "We didn't mean to anger you. Please don't tell Lady Jewel; she'll punish us terribly."

"As she should," the queen's voice snapped. **"I told her this library would be trouble. I don't stand for disobedient SilkWings in *my* Hive. Who else is with you?"**

Cricket squeezed her eyes shut, as though the darkness around her could get any darker.

"No one, Your Majesty," said Tau.

"My cousin Morpho came to scold us earlier," Cinnabar offered. "But he left a little while ago."

"Blue wings," said the queen suspiciously. **"I thought I saw blue wings."**

"That would be Morpho," Cinnabar said. "Or the blankets we sometimes use up there — do you want me to show those to you?"

"No." The shell of the dragon that held the queen hissed. **"This is a waste of time. You, take these two back to Lady Jewel and tell her I said to punish them severely."**

"Sorry again, Your Majesty," Tau said. Cricket tried to figure out how many talonsteps were leaving the library.

How many were left? Was the queen still inside all of them? Would anyone lock the door again? Would the queen leave guards on the library? How long did they have to wait before it was safe to come out?

The tramping of most of the feet faded away, but she could still hear claws scraping across the floor. Someone was still out there.

It felt as though a long time passed, but Sundew didn't open the door of the book drop, and Cricket figured she would know when it was safe to do that. She had just shifted to lean against Blue's shoulder when she heard running steps outside.

"Your Majesty, are you still there?" said a voice.

"Yes," Wasp answered coldly, sounding as if she was standing directly on the other side of the wall from Cricket. **"What is it?"**

"We've had a tip that Lady Scarab is here in Jewel Hive — and she may be hiding another dragon in her mansion."

"Lady Scarab," the queen's voice hissed. "**She *would*. Let's go pay Lady Scarab a visit.**"

Their talonsteps crashed out of the library, and Cricket looked up so quickly her snout knocked into Blue's chin.

"They're talking about Katydid," she whispered. "They're going to arrest my sister!"

CHAPTER 13

Cricket tried to scramble downward but accidentally started a cascade of books.

"Ow!" Sundew whispered from below her. "Quit that! Stop moving right now!"

"I have to get to Katydid," Cricket whispered back, her wings bent awkwardly against the curving walls.

"To do what?" Sundew demanded. "There's nothing you can do to help her."

"I could try to warn her!"

"Won't Queen Wasp have jumped into Katydid already, now that she knows where she is?" Blue whispered.

"Maybe not." Cricket tried to edge down a bit farther. "Sometimes it seems like she needs to know who a dragon is or see her before she can get inside her head."

"So she'll jump into Scarab," Sundew pointed out, "take one look at your sister, jump into her, and off they go. There's no way you can get there in time."

"Couldn't I try?" Cricket pleaded. She thought for a moment. "Wait, I don't need your permission. You've already decided you're not going to help me. So why should I listen to you?" She started scrambling down the column again, kicking more books aside.

"Argh, stop!" Sundew said, squishing herself to one side to get out of Cricket's way. "Listen, I'm not going to help your tribe because they're a lost cause *and* they deserve everything they get! But you're not like them. You can join our side and be safe."

"As long as I forget about Katydid," Cricket said, "and let you hurt a whole lot of dragons who never fought in any war against you. No, thank you." She wrestled Sundew's tail out of her way and shoved the door open, tumbling out into the library in a small avalanche of books. The front lobby of the library was deserted, the main doors standing wide open.

The door on the column opposite hers snuck open a crack and Swordtail's snout poked out. "Oh, thank goodness," he said. "Does Sundew think it's safe to come out? This guy is insufferable even in total silence. OW." He twisted around to glare at the blue tail point that was jabbing him in the head.

"I'm telling you," Sundew said, climbing out behind Cricket, "it's not going to do any good to go watch your sister get arrested. It'll just upset you, and you might get caught."

"I'm going anyway," Cricket said, starting toward the courtyard.

"And I'm going with her," said Blue. He clambered out of the book drop and started shoveling books back into it. "I'm going wherever Cricket goes."

Sundew stamped her foot in frustration. "All right, fine! Let me get my stupid cape." She stormed off to the upper level.

Cricket came back to help Blue shoulder the door of the book drop closed with all the books inside. "Good idea," she said to him. "In case we need these hiding spots again."

"Oh — right," he said. "Yes. Absolutely that."

She couldn't help smiling at him. "You were trying to save the librarians some work, weren't you?"

"They have enough mess to clean up," he said sheepishly, waving his wings at the rest of the library, where boxes of books lay tumbled on their sides, a few shelves had been knocked completely over, and it looked as if everything on the desks that wasn't nailed down had been thrown around.

"Where are we going?" Swordtail asked as Sundew came flying back toward them. "Ow AGAIN!" he yelped as Morpho fell out of the book drop and squashed his tail.

"To get Cricket arrested, as far as I can tell," Sundew grumbled, throwing the saffron-colored silk cape over her wings.

"I have to get home," Morpho said. "My dad worries if I'm out too late."

"I want to meet *everyone* in the Jewel Hive Chrysalis *today*," Sundew said to him. "Outside the Hive, next to the farthest stall of the Glitterbazaar, when the sun is at its highest point."

He nodded, his eyes shining, and flew off.

Cricket was already leading the way up to the higher levels, thinking about sunset. *That's how long we have until Belladonna's deadline. We have to bring her something real by then, or HiveWings will start to die.* Her heart thudded painfully in her chest. She liked Sundew — most of the time — and being with Sundew had made her start thinking all LeafWings were like that. But when she stopped to remember Sundew's parents, Belladonna and Hemlock, she felt an almost crushing fear for the rest of her tribe.

The higher levels were the busiest at this time of night, as HiveWings swarmed from one party to another, always rushing to make sure they didn't miss anything, to make sure they made at least an appearance everywhere. Many of them had their most beautiful SilkWings along with them, although at this hour Cricket could see that the rules were more relaxed. SilkWings and HiveWings chatted to one another as they walked or browsed the appetizer tables;

SilkWings joined the dances in the ballrooms, laughing and singing along.

There are HiveWings here who see the SilkWings as equals, she was sure of it. HiveWings who might be willing to join a revolution to stop the queen and change the rules of this world. If they could . . . if they were given the chance before the LeafWings started a new war.

Lady Scarab's mansion was one of the only quiet ones up here — no music rang from the windows, no dragons fluttered in and out. But a squad of HiveWings were gathered on her front steps, some of them tapping their claws impatiently.

"Open this door, Scarab!" the queen roared from inside one of the soldiers.

A short way down the street, Cricket ducked into a party that overflowed the edges of an elegant courtyard. Nearly invisible strands of silk draped from the hedges and arches and gazebo, hung with tiny firefly sculptures, each one with a small dot of flamesilk inside so the party seemed to be dotted with real fireflies. A trio of SilkWings played quiet string instruments in a corner. Several of the guests turned around with disapproving looks when they heard the shouting at Scarab's house, then turned back quickly, making their faces blank, when they realized who was doing the shouting.

Cricket slipped through the crowd and picked up a fizzy coconut-scented drink from one of the tables, trying to look as though she went to parties all the time, this was perfectly normal, parties were easy and fun, ha ha, yes, hooray for socializing, that was absolutely a thing she liked to do.

The other three stayed close to her, looking possibly even more conspicuous than she did — wide-eyed Blue, scowling Sundew, and twitchy Swordtail — but the crush of dragons made it unlikely anyone would stop and examine them closely.

"Try this one," Cricket heard a SilkWing say, scooping a glass of something fuchsia from one of the many sparkling punch bowls scattered on tables around the party. The HiveWing he handed it to tasted the drink and made a face.

"SCARAB!" bellowed the queen, and Cricket saw everyone at the party trying to hide their reactions — irritation here, fear over there, that one perhaps glee, those two definitely curiosity. The soldiers pounded on the door with talons and tails and spiky clubs. "Open this door or I'll —"

The door flew open and one of the soldiers nearly fell inside. Lady Scarab glared out at the knot of dragons on her doorstep. Cricket had to crane her neck to see the elderly dragon around a few other partygoers. She wasn't the only one; now several guests were staring openly down the street at the commotion.

"Or you'll *what*?" Lady Scarab demanded.

"Oh no," whispered a HiveWing standing near Cricket.

"Do you think she's going to do that smell thing?" whispered another. Her friend nodded. "Come on, let's sneak out before it becomes unbearable up here." The two HiveWings wove away toward the ramps in a hurry. Cricket saw a crimson dragon by the food table — probably the host — glance despairingly around as a few others sidled off, too.

"Who else is here?" the queen demanded.

"A young friend of mine," Lady Scarab snapped. "She's asleep, like a sensible dragon, so take your goons and shut up and go away."

Small gasps sounded from around the party, and Cricket saw one SilkWing accidentally drop her glass with a tiny smash.

"Bring her out."

"Wasp. She's none of your concern. Surely you have more important things to do; just leave her be."

The white-eyed solder hissed and lashed his tail. **"Prove to me she's not the traitor we're looking for."**

"She's not!" Scarab snapped, exasperated. "Haven't you taken enough from me, Wasp? This dragon has done you no harm."

Scarab is arguing with her, Cricket suddenly realized with a jolt. *She's arguing with Queen Wasp. She's saying no to her.*

Queen Wasp wouldn't cause a scene like this if she could avoid it.

That must mean . . . she can't control Lady Scarab.

Scarab is like me. She's free from the mind control!

"Who is in there, Scarab?" the queen demanded. All of the soldiers' eyes turned white. The party suddenly went very quiet behind Cricket.

Uh-oh.

She darted a glance sideways. The HiveWing beside her had white eyes as well. Cricket guessed everyone at the party had been taken over. The SilkWings were still murmuring to one another, but their voices slowly faded to silence.

Cricket kept her head down, hoping her eyes were hidden by the folds of the blue veil around her horns. All the HiveWings had their heads turned toward Scarab's house, alert and coiled like angry snakes. So far they were a threat, not yet a weapon. As long as she stayed still, with luck no one would look closer at her.

Her heart constricted, eating all the air in her chest.

"You stay out of my house, Wasp," Lady Scarab said furiously. "You have no right to poke your snout in —"

"I have every right. I am your queen." The voice came from all the HiveWings on the street now. It was chilling to hear it so close, the breath of all the stolen guests shivering across Cricket's wings. On Scarab's steps, two of the

HiveWings stepped forward and menacing stingers slid out from under their claws.

"You're a creepy old bat!" Scarab shouted. "Your mother would hate to see what you've done with her tribe!"

"Lucky for us that she's dead, then."

Scarab hissed at the stingers reaching toward her. Suddenly the soldiers staggered back, their eyes watering. All the dragons on her front steps covered their snouts.

A moment later, the smell rolled over the party. Cricket had heard of dragons with Scarab's power, and she'd even smelled a fraction of it once when Scarab was annoyed by some dragonets in her way at the market. But this had to be the full-force weaponized version of it, like dead rotting things pickled in sulfur. It made her want to claw off her own nose. She saw the white eyes flicker out of the faces around her; she guessed the queen couldn't stand to experience it through so many dragons. Several of the party guests dropped their drinks and ran for the stairs.

"I will come here and kill you myself if I have to," Wasp snarled from one of the soldiers' mouths.

"Ha," said Lady Scarab. "Doing your own dirty work? Doesn't sound like you, Wasp."

"Lady Scarab."

Cricket felt cracks shiver across her heart. Katydid had

appeared beside Scarab, touching the older dragon's shoulder gently.

Scarab's wings drooped. "Idiot child. I could have kept you safe."

"I don't want you to get in trouble for me," Katydid said. "There's no reason to. I haven't done anything wrong. I'll come with you willingly," she said to the guards.

"Hm. Familiar, but not the dragon I'm looking for. What an interesting mystery," said the queen. **"Some relation to my missing friend, I'm guessing?"**

Lady Scarab only glared at her, but Katydid dropped her gaze to her feet.

"Well," said the queen, **"perhaps we can find a use for her."**

Katydid looked up again, and her eyes were blank as the faces of the moons, empty like the husks of spider-eaten grubs.

"Nice try, Lady Scarab," the queen said with Katydid's mouth, Katydid's voice, Katydid's mind. **"I'm sure I'll be seeing you again soon."**

And then Katydid stepped out of the house, joined the group of HiveWing soldiers, and marched away.

— CHAPTER 14 —

Lady Scarab slammed the door of her mansion hard enough to make the firefly lanterns rattle all over the courtyard down the street.

The trio of SilkWings quickly started the music again, and the babble of conversation rose, a little strained and a little higher-pitched than before. A few more guests made excuses to the host, who was stirring a pale green tea dejectedly, and vanished toward the ramps to find safer, better-smelling parties.

Sundew came up beside Cricket, twitching her cape a little closer around her. "I don't understand how you all live like this," she whispered.

"We don't have a choice," Cricket whispered back. "But did you see Scarab fighting back? Don't you think she must be like me? Maybe she knows how the mind control works!" *And if she does, maybe she can help me save Katydid. That's*

the only thing I can do — there's no way to rescue Katydid
unless I can free her from the mind control.

"Oh no," Sundew muttered. "You want to go over there. To the house your queen literally just raided."

"So she's hardly likely to come back right away, right?" Cricket said.

Sundew shook her head and moved to one of the bowls, scooping a dark purple liquid out of it and sniffing it suspiciously. "I should go find my parents. I have to tell them that our plan didn't work." She sighed. "The Chrysalis knew nothing helpful about the mind control. Nor do they seem like particularly useful allies, but I'll ask Belladonna what she wants me to do with them."

"Wait," Cricket said, feeling a surge of panic. "Sundew, please. We still have until sunset. Don't go yet. Give me the rest of today to try to find some answers."

The party host had found some perfume and was wandering the courtyard, trying to inconspicuously spritz it everywhere. Sundew wrinkled her snout at him. "Fine. You can try," she whispered. "But don't get your hopes up. And you can't take Blue to Scarab's house with you. We don't know if we can trust that old HiveWing, and he's too valuable to risk."

Blue protested, but Cricket agreed with her — she didn't

know how Lady Scarab would react to Blue, or how she felt about SilkWings in general. She was the only wealthy HiveWing Cricket knew of who had no SilkWing servants. Cricket got the impression she disliked them only about as much as she disliked all dragons. But Lady Scarab was very unpredictable, and Cricket didn't want to put Blue in any danger.

"All right," she whispered. "If I don't come back before the party ends, meet me at the statue in the Glitterbazaar."

She turned and touched one of Blue's talons lightly with hers, wishing she could hug him, but not sure whether the rules could bend quite that far.

"Be careful," he said softly as she slipped away.

The guests who remained were valiantly trying to ignore Lady Scarab's residence and the odor that still lingered around it. Still, Cricket was afraid that knocking on the front door might catch the attention of the more gossipy dragons, so she tried walking in the opposite direction and circling through the streets until she reached the side of the mansion, where a smaller door was set into the wall.

She knocked nervously and stood for a long, anxious moment, gazing up at the weathered treestuff that formed the outside of the mansion. Most wealthy dragons kept their homes neatly maintained and constantly updated with new features, but the green jade beetles inlaid in even rows looked as though they had been put in decades ago, maybe when the house was first built. Some of them were even missing, although Cricket couldn't tell whether they'd been pried loose and stolen or whether they'd fallen out and nobody cared.

The door swung open abruptly, making Cricket jump.

"No!" Lady Scarab barked, and slammed the door shut again.

"Wait!" Cricket knocked more firmly. "Lady Scarab, wait!"

The door flew open midknock and Cricket nearly rapped the elderly dragon on the nose.

"Go away!" Lady Scarab shouted.

"It's me," Cricket said quickly, shoving her veil aside to reveal her face. "Please, Lady Scarab."

"Oh, by all the stupid moons," Scarab growled. She grabbed Cricket by one of the scarves and yanked her inside, almost throttling her in the process.

Cricket stumbled into a poorly lit kitchen, bare and cold. One flamesilk lamp sat alone on the central table, its light dim as though the thread had almost faded completely. Next to it were two plates, neatly stacked, and a small glass jar of pale lavender sugar cubes. In the sink she spotted the bones of a bird, but there was no other food in sight. The walls were empty except for two small paintings on either side of the stove: one a lemon tree, the other an orange tree.

Trees? Cricket thought, startled. No one was allowed to make art with trees in it. No one was allowed to *have* art with trees in it. She squinted at them and saw the spidery cracks in the canvas. Maybe they were quite old, from before the laws about trees in art. Still, it was bold of Scarab to have kept them.

"Come on, you nuisance," Scarab muttered, grabbing the lamp and stomping past Cricket into the next room. This one was much bigger, reaching all the way to the back wall of the mansion, where tall sliding glass doors led to a balcony overlooking the moonlit savanna. Perhaps it had been a ballroom once, or at least intended for hosting grand parties, but now it felt like a giant empty terrarium with only one seed rattling around inside it.

It was also cold and sparsely decorated, especially for a dragon who seemed as rich as Lady Scarab. A polished old wood bookcase filled the opposite wall, lined with books that looked as though they might crumble if you actually touched them. One dark green floor pillow was set by the balcony doors, as though the only place she wanted to sit was near the exit, with a view of the stars.

Lady Scarab set the lamp on the low table and sat down on the pillow, leaving Cricket standing awkwardly in the middle of the room.

"Well?" the old dragon demanded. "After all this trouble, at least tell me you brought the Book."

Surprised, Cricket said, "My friend has it. What do you know about the Book?"

"Not enough," Lady Scarab growled. "I've wanted to get my claws on it for years. I assume you read it. What happens next? Say the words 'Wasp dies slowly and horribly' and I'll make you my heir."

Cricket was startled into almost laughing. "No, no," she said, recovering quickly. "It's not like that. That's the thing: there are no more predictions in it. Clearsight only saw a few hundred years into the future — there's nothing about now, nothing about the last thousand years. Queen Wasp has been lying to us."

Lady Scarab's eyes were like small dark coals, with flickers of dark red in their depths. Those eyes pinned Cricket to the bare floor for a long, agonizing moment.

"What?" Scarab spat.

"The Tree Wars were all a lie; Clearsight never saw that. The SilkWing queen giving up her throne so her tribe would bow to Queen Wasp . . . that wasn't in there, either."

Scarab breathed deeply in and out through her nose. "I suppose," she said icily, "there wasn't a list of the HiveWing queen succession line, either."

"N-no," Cricket said. "What's that?"

"A list, allegedly, of who should be queen and who should succeed her, from Clearsight's time all the way until now." Lady

Scarab let out her breath again in a long hiss through her teeth. "So my mother was lying about the Book, too. And so was my sister. Both lying, in fact, about the fact that my sister Cochineal had to be queen. I suppose Mother realized she was always a much better liar than I was. The most essential quality for a queen who had to rule by deceiving her entire tribe about their most sacred artifact. What a lovely, lovely royal family we are."

She picked up a paintbrush from a tray beside the pillow, and Cricket realized there was a small easel there as well. The half-finished painting, as far as she could see, was of a wasp being eaten by ants. She shivered.

Lady Scarab shoved her spectacles higher up her nose and squinted at Cricket. "The queen would very much like to kill you, you know. Tell me, why aren't you hiding in some distant corner of the continent?"

"I have some questions —" Cricket said.

"Ah," Lady Scarab interrupted. "Curiosity. That never ends badly. Carry on."

"The queen can't mind-control me," Cricket blurted.

"Yes," said Lady Scarab. "I gathered that from the you-not-marching-yourself-off-to-jail-right-now."

"But why? Why can't the queen mind-control you?" Cricket asked. "Or me?"

"I have no idea." Lady Scarab waved the paintbrush at Cricket. "Next question."

"How can you have no idea?" Cricket asked. "Don't you know how it works?"

"Apparently I am not among those blessed with the secrets of my noble family," Lady Scarab snarked. "In any case, nobody knows why Wasp can do what she does. No other dragon has ever done it before."

"Ever?" Cricket echoed. "In all of Pantalan history? Are you sure?"

"Of course I'm sure." The royal HiveWing stabbed her paintbrush into a puddle of red paint and started adding thin lines of blood coming out of the wasp in her painting. Cricket had a feeling this particular piece of art might be even more poorly received than the trees in the kitchen. "I've got history books going back centuries. I've traced the family trees as far out as I can. Not a single HiveWing with mind-control powers, all the way back to Clearsight, as far as I could find. And it certainly didn't come from her SilkWing husbands."

"SilkWing?" Cricket said, extremely startled. *"Husbands?"*

"Yes, of course," Lady Scarab snapped. "Maybe they weren't called SilkWings back then. ShimmerWings or Flibbertigibbets or something in the old language, I don't know. But Clearsight married one, and then another one when the first one died, and had an alarming number of dragonets with each one, and then their dragonets and their dragonets' dragonets kept going, marrying Ye Olde SilkWings or what have you, until there was enough of them to be considered their own tribe. HiveWings. Stupid menacing name, if you ask me. It was only about five hundred years ago that we officially split into two separate tribes, you know. My charming great-great-grandmother was the queen who ordered no more mingling of the bloodlines. She was a nightmare."

"We're related to SilkWings?" Cricket said again. "Really?"

Lady Scarab squinted at her with concern. "Oh dear, are you thick?" she asked. "I thought Katydid said you were rather clever. It is *perfectly obvious* that HiveWings must have started with Clearsight marrying a SilkWing."

Cricket did feel like rather an idiot. In her defense, history was the most neglected subject at Terrarium Academy. "Well," she said indignantly, "it is also *perfectly obvious* that HiveWing books leave that out on *purpose* because they don't want any of us to *know that*."

"True," said Lady Scarab, settling back to her painting, which was getting gorier by the moment. "That was probably also my great-great-grandmother's idea. Oooo, she was a horror show."

"Did any of Clearsight's children inherit her prophecy powers?" Cricket asked. She'd always wondered about that. HiveWings had all sorts of weird powers pop up throughout the tribe, but nothing like Clearsight's. The mind control had seemed the closest, to her, being at least kind of mental.

"Not according to the records." Scarab coughed violently. "But then, if I were Clearsight, I'd tell my kids to keep that information to themselves. If you know the future, but no one else *knows* you know the future, you've got an advantage, see? HA!" She started coughing again, finally sputtering to a wheezing stop. "Maybe I am related to my family after all."

Cricket started to pace up and down the long, empty room. Through the haze of drizzling rain outside, she thought she could see a faint line of gray along the horizon, which meant sunrise was coming, which meant sunset was getting ever closer.

"So why doesn't the mind control work on us?" she said. "Let's think. Do we have anything in common? Is there anyone else who's free of it?"

"Wasp's sisters," answered Lady Scarab. "And Jewel, although Wasp has threatened her with it a few times."

"Threatened her with it?" Cricket echoed, pausing for a moment. "Like . . . she *could* mind-control her, if she wanted to?"

Lady Scarab shrugged helpfully.

"Hmm." Cricket went back to pacing. "Do you know anything about a home for old dragons in Tsetse Hive? Where they're kept because none of them are controllable?"

"No," Lady Scarab said, narrowing her eyes. "But I have noticed that I am the oldest dragon I know. All of my friends started dying off or vanishing during the Tree Wars. Most of them were loudly against the war, so I wasn't too surprised. But some of them went funny before they went — saying weird things that weren't like themselves, strange flutters like curtains in their eyes."

Cricket tipped her head to the side. "As though their eyes were flashing white, then back to normal?" Scarab nodded. "I saw that happen to a dragon, too." She described the dragon she'd seen out the window when she was two.

"Charming story," said Lady Scarab. She added some more red paint fountaining out of the wasp's head.

"Maybe what we saw were Wasp's experiments," Cricket said slowly. "Maybe she was testing out whether she could control those dragons, but she couldn't for some reason. Or maybe she couldn't yet — maybe her power was still getting stronger at that point."

"Makes no sense." Scarab jabbed the paintbrush at Cricket again. "HiveWings are born with their powers. They don't wander in fifty years later. Why couldn't she do any of this when she was younger? Those forty or so blissful years before she became queen? Not that my sister was any picnic as a ruler, but at least she wasn't a dictatorial zombie-making maniac."

"And why doesn't it work on us?" Cricket said again. She sat down opposite Lady Scarab and tried not to look at the painting of the dying wasp, which now looked as though it might drown in blood before the ants could eat it. "I — I have one theory. About me, anyway. I don't know if it's possible, but I wondered maybe . . ."

"Spit it out," Lady Scarab ordered.

"Could I be half SilkWing?" Cricket asked. "Katydid said my parents aren't my real parents and so I thought, maybe one of my parents was a SilkWing and his blood or her blood is why the mind control doesn't —"

"No," Lady Scarab said with a bitter little laugh.

"No?"

"No, you're not half SilkWing."

Cricket blinked. "How do you know? Maybe you are, too. Maybe that's —"

"I *am* getting worried about your brain, dragonet. I knew that school would be worthless for you, but I didn't think all your mental functions would atrophy so quickly." Lady Scarab set down the paintbrush and clasped her front talons together, leaning toward Cricket. "I know you are not half SilkWing, because I know both your parents, and they are HiveWings through and through, zombie eyes and all."

"You *know* them?" Cricket cried, leaping to her feet. "They're still alive? Who are they? Why didn't they keep me?"

"One of them did," said Lady Scarab. "She just couldn't tell anyone you were hers. I can't believe you haven't figured it out before now."

Cricket felt as if the Hive was falling in on her, slowly, level by level, like in a dream.

"Katydid isn't your sister, little snail. She's your mother."

CHAPTER 15

It felt like the entire world flipped over. It felt like someone picked up the Hive, turned it over, and shook it really hard until all the pieces fell out. Except one, and that one was the heart of everything.

"*Katydid,*" she said softly. "My mother. Katydid is my mother. *Katydid.*"

"I gather this is going to go on for a while," Scarab muttered, producing a new easel from behind the pillow. On this one, a horde of shiny green beetles was dragging a dying wasp into a dark hole where little eyes and teeth glinted from the shadows.

"I wish she had told me. Why didn't she tell me? She knew I could keep a secret." Cricket flicked her tail back and forth. "She just *lied* to me. Was she planning to hide the truth from me my whole life?"

"Would it have made any difference, knowing the truth?" Scarab asked sharply.

"Yes!" Cricket said. "It would have made *everything* make more sense. Well . . . all right, I would have had a few questions."

"Really. You." Lady Scarab raised her eyebrows.

"But at least it would have explained a whole lot of things. Oh. *Oh.* That's why Mom — not-Mom — Cadelle hates me," Cricket said. There *were* answers to all her unanswerable questions: the way her parents fought, why they barely looked at her, the reason Katydid always looked sad. "That's why Katydid always took care of me. Oh my goodness, that's what Cadelle meant whenever she said, 'You're no daughter of mine.' It was *true.*"

"Lucky for you," Scarab snorted. "That one has a personality like sandpaper."

Cricket thought this was rather funny coming from Lady Scarab, but she didn't point that out.

"How did they keep it a secret?" she wondered. She tried to puzzle through what they would have had to do. It was possible no one had noticed that Katydid was with egg; many dragons grew plumper in the rainy months when there was more food and less opportunity for outdoor flying. And Katydid was good at keeping secrets — obviously.

But what did she do once she had the egg? All HiveWing eggs in each Hive were kept in a central nest until they hatched. Maybe Cadelle simply had to present herself at the nest with Katydid's egg, claiming it was hers. It would be marked as hers, protected as the dragonet inside grew, and then returned to Cadelle a day before it was due to hatch.

"It's so hard to imagine Cadelle agreeing to a lie like that," Cricket said aloud.

"She didn't want to," said Lady Scarab. "There was an enormous fight when she found out Katydid was hiding your egg. If it was up to your delightful grandmother, they would have taken it out to the ocean and dropped you on a rock somewhere."

This Cricket *could* imagine, very easily. Although it was so strange to hear Cadelle referred to as her grandmother. *I was still her family, even if I wasn't her daughter. But my existence was against the rules. I represented Katydid lying to her and Queen Wasp being furious if she found out. Having me around put Cadelle at risk . . . she must have seen danger and crime and disorder and lies that could ruin her every time she looked at me.*

"In the end, Katydid agreed to sneak the egg into the Cicada Hive Nest, so it could come back official and approved instead of you being a secret forever. And Cadelle agreed to pretend it was hers." Lady Scarab grinned with all of her teeth. "I might have helped with that little compromise."

Cricket wondered whether Lady Scarab's "help" came in the form of threats or offers to help Cadelle social climb. "Weren't there official records, though?" she asked.

"I helped with those, too." Lady Scarab looked extremely pleased with herself. "A little bribery, a little distraction, a forged document, and then you were Cadelle's and everything was in order."

"But why would you help my sis — I mean, Katydid — at all?" Cricket asked, guessing part of the answer already. "Did you . . . did you know my dad?"

Lady Scarab's grin disappeared like waves pulling back off the beach before a tsunami. She stared down at her painting for a long moment, then set down the paintbrush and heaved herself upright with a growl.

Cricket moved out of the way as the old dragon stomped over to the bookshelf. Lady Scarab pulled out an old, dark green book and flipped it open. Inside, the pages had been carved away to leave a hollow for a small painting.

The dragon in the portrait had kind eyes; that was the first thing Cricket noticed. He wore glasses, just like her. His scales were a warm orange color, except for his wings, which were dark red, with spots of black scales here and there. Some of them even looked like ink blots, like hers did. He was holding a book, which made Cricket want to cry.

"Who is he?" she whispered, touching the painting lightly with one claw. *Definitely a HiveWing. So I'm really not a hybrid.*

"Malachite," said Lady Scarab. "My secretary, back when I was still allegedly the minister of education. Brilliant, talented, made excellent coffee, full of exciting ideas. The first dragon in years who gave me hope for the future of our tribe." She sighed. "It was my fault, really. Queen Wasp has always hated me. I should have known better than to let her see there was a dragon I cared about. To spite me, she forbade his marriage to the dragon he fell in love with."

"Katydid," Cricket said.

"Yes. And then she took him away from me, before he even knew you existed. He works for her now."

"He's really still alive?" Cricket whispered, looking up at her.

"In a sense," Scarab said bitterly. "She parades him past me whenever she can, always with those hateful white eyes. I don't know if he ever gets to be himself. I haven't seen him with his own eyes since the day she took him over and summoned him to Wasp Hive." She hissed. "I have to pretend like I don't care. If she doesn't get a reaction from me, maybe one day she'll lose interest and let him go."

That's why Lady Scarab has no servants, Cricket realized. *That's why she's always alone — so there's no one Wasp can hurt to get to her.*

"Is that what's going to happen to Katydid?" she asked.

"I hope not," said Scarab. "Queen Wasp usually gets bored rather quickly. If Katydid can't lead her to you, she won't have much use for her."

"I wish I could rescue them," Cricket said, twisting her talons together.

"Well, you can't," Lady Scarab pointed out. "Because Wasp can control them anytime she wants, and she'll just march them right back to prison."

A wave of anger rushed through Cricket, strong and sudden. "There *has* to be a way to stop her."

Scarab snapped the cover closed over the portrait of Malachite. "I was hoping you'd found one in the Book. But if there are no more predictions, then it's all chaos." She waved her talons in the air. "Anything could happen! She doesn't have secret knowledge of the future after all." Scarab chuckled. "No wonder she wants you dead."

Cricket ran her claws along the bookshelf, thinking. She still didn't have an answer to the mind-control question. She didn't know if the HiveWings could be saved from it. But she did have one thing: the truth about the Book.

Katydid should have trusted me with the truth about her and Malachite.

My tribe deserves the truth, too. They need to know that Queen Wasp has been lying to them.

Cricket looked around the room. If this was her last day in the Hives, she had to use it well. She couldn't just look for answers anymore; she had to make sure other dragons also knew them.

"Lady Scarab," she said. "Can I borrow a paintbrush?"

Tsetse Hive

Beetle Lake

Vinegaroon
Hive

Hornet Hive

Cicada Hive

Mantis
Hive

PART THREE
THE QUEEN'S SECRETS

—— CHAPTER 16 ——

Sundew didn't like it, and so Swordtail didn't like it, either, although Cricket suspected he would have been all for it otherwise. Blue loved the idea, though, and that was what she cared about.

"This is way too dangerous," Sundew protested.

"Exactly," said Swordtail.

"Queen Wasp may already suspect we're in Jewel Hive; this will just prove it to her," Sundew pointed out. "It'll be snake eyes and everyone talking at the same time again in a heartbeat, and then we'll be surrounded, and then we'll be caught, and then *none* of our plans will have a chance."

"None of them!" Swordtail said, waving his wings around dramatically. "Because we'll be in the clutches of zombie HiveWings!"

"All right, simmer down," Sundew said, rolling her eyes.

They were huddled inside one of the indoor stalls of the Glitterbazaar, not far from the Salvation Statue. This one sold books, wonderful beautiful books with gold leaf on the spines and feathery edges to the silk pages. Cricket couldn't stop picking them up, just to feel something safe and beloved in her talons again. A part of her wished she could abandon this plan, crawl under one of the tables, and read all the books in this stall for the rest of her life instead.

Hanging from the top of the doorway, wind chimes with little hummingbirds dangling from them sounded in the breeze. Dawn was coming, and the market was virtually empty. Even on the upper levels, most of the dragons they'd seen had been dragging themselves sleepily off to bed.

"I know," Cricket said. "But I have to do something. It's no use knowing the truth if everyone else still believes the lies. My tribe needs to know that Queen Wasp is lying to them. Maybe I can't set them free from the mind control yet, but knowing the truth about the Book . . ." She looked down at the scarf she'd been twisting between her claws. "I think knowing the truth is the first step toward their freedom. I hope."

"I hope so, too," Blue agreed. "I mean, imagine you've only been told one thing your whole life. Imagine you don't even know it *could* be a lie." He hesitated. "This is going to be hard for dragons to hear."

"What are we supposed to do with all this?" Sundew asked, flicking her claws at the stacks of silk paper that Cricket had taken from a nearby stationery stall.

"We're going to write out Clearsight's letter from the end of her book," Cricket said. "Over and over again, as many copies as we can make. At the top, write 'This is what the book really says' and at the bottom write 'There are no more predictions. Queen Wasp is lying.'"

Swordtail groaned and flopped his head down onto his talons. *"Wriiiiiiting,"* he whined. "That sounds like homework. Nobody said the revolution would involve *homework*."

Sundew whacked him on the head with one of her wings. "You are lucky that you *can* write," she said. "We were told that SilkWings weren't allowed to go to school."

"What?!" Cricket yelped. She couldn't imagine being forbidden to go to school. "That would be cruel and awful and barbaric!"

The LeafWing shot her an amused look. "Well, exactly," she said.

"Sounds all right to me," Swordtail muttered, but he accepted the inkwell and sheaf of papers with only a little more grumbling.

Cricket made the first copies, as she was the fastest writer, and then they all copied from those, working as quickly as they could. When they had well over a hundred and the sun was starting to sidle in through the far windows, she stopped them and collected the papers.

"Now you have to go," she said.

"Go where?" Blue asked.

"To hide for the day," Cricket answered. "Somewhere far away from Jewel Hive. I'm doing the next part by myself."

"Then I'm going back out to look for Luna," Swordtail said.

"While I get to meet with the Chrysalis," Sundew sighed.

Blue took one of Cricket's talons in his. "No way. I got you into this mess. I'm not leaving you alone to deal with it."

She shook her head. "You didn't get me into this mess, Blue. Queen Wasp did this. She kept my parents apart and she stole my father. She used the Book to make herself powerful and lied to the entire tribe to do it. You helped me find the truth, and now I have to help my tribe the same way."

"Technically *I* helped you find the truth," Sundew observed, "since it was *my* idea to steal the Book in the first place."

"I, too, have been important to this whole — everything," Swordtail chimed in.

Cricket put her wings around Blue, awkwardly now that his own wings were in the way, and hugged him close. "You have to stay safe to help the SilkWings and the LeafWings," she said. "But the HiveWings are my responsibility. All right?"

"Also," Sundew said, "it's better if only one of us gets caught. Then the others can maybe rescue her. *Maybe*," she repeated, wagging one claw in Cricket's face. "But also MAYBE NOT, so don't get caught."

"I won't," Cricket said. "I'll try. Go hide. I'll meet you by the last stall outside before sunset."

"We can go look for Luna together," Swordtail said, nudging Blue's side. "We can split up and cover a lot more of the bay with two of us — three if Sundew helps. Maybe she's hurt and stuck on an island. Or in a cave and can't find us. Please help me, Blue. Luna and I need your help."

Cricket guessed that Swordtail meant it, but that he was also trying to give Blue a way to be able to leave her — by reminding him of another dragon who needed his help even more than she did.

Blue opened and closed his talons, looking at them as if he was hoping they'd tell him what to do.

"I will, but . . . Cricket," Blue said woefully. "I don't want to leave you."

"I know," she said, her voice catching in her throat. "But you can understand what I'm feeling, right? You can imagine how important this is to me and . . . and how important *you* are to me."

He blinked back tears and leaned closer so their noses touched, and then Swordtail dragged him away and the three of them were gone, Blue still looking over his shoulder at the last moment.

It was hard to watch them hurry away through the displays of the Glitterbazaar. It was really hard to stop herself from shouting, "Wait, come back! I don't want to do this by myself! I'm actually terrified!"

But she took deep breaths and stayed quiet. And as soon as they were out of sight, she set out to complete the next part of her plan.

She knew the queen would tear down anything she put up as fast as possible, so she focused on quantity — as many messages in as many places as she could. Lady Scarab's largest pot of paint was the bright pink color of hibiscus flowers, so that was what she used on every poster, every open surface, every blank unguarded wall. She especially enjoyed painting over the Wanted posters, covering her own face with tall pink letters.

THE QUEEN IS LYING TO YOU

CLEARSIGHT NEVER PREDICTED THE TREE WARS

CLEARSIGHT NEVER SAID THE OTHER TRIBES SHOULD BOW TO THE HIVEWINGS

EVERYTHING QUEEN WASP SAYS ABOUT THE BOOK IS A LIE

CLEARSIGHT'S PREDICTIONS ENDED A THOUSAND YEARS AGO

THE QUEEN IS LYING TO YOU

THE QUEEN IS LYING TO YOU

THE QUEEN IS LYING TO YOU

She slid the paper with Clearsight's letter on it under doors and scattered them through the parks. She left one on top of the book the Clearsight statue was reading outside the library. She couldn't bring herself to do anything else to that statue, but she had no trouble defacing the Salvation Statue in the Glitterbazaar, scrawling LIAR in enormous pink letters all over the queen's face and wings and then WASP IS LYING around the base.

The sun was well above the horizon and the streets were starting to fill when she ran out of paint. A few dragonets on their way to school saw her slipping the papers under doors and asked what they were, so she gave them one.

"This is the truth," she said. "I've seen the Book of Clearsight."

They gazed up at her, wide-eyed, three tiny HiveWings and two wingless SilkWings.

"Really?" said one of them. "Is it amazing?"

"It is amazing, but not the way you'd think," she said. She tapped the paper. "This is what it really says."

They all gathered around to sound out the words together, and she hurried away to the next level, wondering how long she had before Queen Wasp saw the messages through some-one's eyes.

Two levels up, a door opened just as she slipped the paper underneath. A startled HiveWing stood there on her way out to work.

"Hey!" said the strange dragon. "Who are you? What's this?"

"It's —" Cricket took a deep breath. *Be brave.* "It's the truth," she said. She picked up the paper and held it out to the dragon. "I thought everyone should know what the Book of Clearsight *really* says."

The dragon's jaw dropped open. "You're the one from the Wanted posters!" She seized the paper from Cricket's talons. "You really did read the Book? By the stars, I've always wanted to know what it says!"

"Me too," Cricket said. "And now I think everyone should know."

She left the HiveWing standing there, reading with shining eyes.

They are listening. They want the truth. Maybe this will work.

But her luck ran out on the way to the water tower, where she had hoped to hide for the day. She was hurrying through the streets, ducking her head to avoid meeting anyone's eyes, when she turned a corner and ran into Cadelle.

"Oh!" Cricket yelped, looking straight into her mother — no, her grandmother's face. "I mean, sorry, sorry, ma'am." She tried to cover her confusion, to bow and turn away and continue on like any other stranger in a hurry.

But Cadelle seized her arm in an iron grip. "You," she snarled. "What are you doing *here*? In *my* Hive? Are you *trying* to get me arrested?" She dragged Cricket through

Dragonfly Square to her house and threw her inside, slamming the door behind them.

Cricket stumbled on the gray silk carpet, trying to put some distance between herself and Cadelle. There was so much in this living room that reminded Cricket of her childhood — the square black marble side tables her mother had taken with her, the ivory reproduction of the Salvation Statue with tiny garnet eyes, the smell of chamomile tea and boiled rabbits coming from the kitchen. Everything in the house was exactly the same as it had been a year ago; every book exactly even with the edge of the shelf, every painting perfectly aligned with the next, Queen Wasp glaring at Lady Jewel, who stared blankly at the most boring Clearsight in portrait history.

Even the terror wasn't entirely new. She'd never been able to predict what Cadelle would do next. She'd always been afraid of something sudden and terrible striking out of the blue.

But this time the room felt colder, the smell of meat stronger, and this time the threat of Queen Wasp poisoned everything. This time, instead of yelling or throwing things, Cadelle might deliver Cricket right into the queen's waiting claws.

"I kept my mouth shut," Cadelle hissed. "I didn't want anyone to know I had anything to do with you. And then you show up here? Did you think I would help you?"

"No!" Cricket rubbed her scales where Cadelle had dug her claws in. "I didn't want to see you at all!"

Cadelle's wings flared. "Then why here — why this Hive, why so close to *my* house? I came here to get away from you!"

"I know," Cricket said. "And I know why. Don't worry, I want to get away from you, too." She took a step toward the door, but Cadelle blocked her path, baring the venomous teeth that neither her child, nor grandchild, had inherited. Cricket had seen her use them a few times to bring down prey, especially larger animals like antelopes or water buffalo.

But she'd also once seen Cadelle bite a dragon . . . a new SilkWing cook who had accidentally burned Cadelle's favorite meal on a bad day. The venom had spread quickly from the wound on his neck, and there had been screaming, and he'd only survived because Father (*Grandfather*) got him to the hospital in time.

Cricket mostly remembered the screaming.

That, and the realization that Cadelle was even more dangerous than she'd thought.

Would she do that to me?

"Just let me go. Pretend you didn't see me," Cricket said. "If we're both lucky, you'll never see me again."

Cadelle frowned. *She's not used to me talking back*, Cricket thought. *She's never seen me try to push her away; she's always been the one doing the pushing.*

"Do you have the Book?" Cadelle asked, her tail lashing.

"No," Cricket answered. "But I've seen it. I've read it, and I know Queen Wasp has been lying to everyone about it."

Cadelle brought her wings in close and squinted at Cricket with her "professor" face. "Is that so? I must say, teaching the history of Pantala feels quite incomplete without a resource like the Book. I've always thought it should be available for study."

"Me too," Cricket said. "Maybe we do have something in common after all."

"You could give me the Book," Cadelle said, advancing toward Cricket. Her teeth seemed to grow longer and sharper as she smiled. "I am actually qualified enough to know what to do with it. It shouldn't be in the talons of some grubby SilkWings."

"I told you I don't have it," Cricket said, backing up until her tail hit the wall behind her and her wings nearly knocked down a map of Pantala. "And I wouldn't give it to you even if I did. You'd probably give it back to Queen Wasp in exchange for an invitation to a party."

Cadelle hissed furiously. "Maybe, but I'd read it first!" she snapped.

"Well, there's a copy of a piece of it on the statue outside the library," Cricket said. "Let me go and you can go read it yourself."

Cadelle suddenly went very still. Outside, Cricket could hear running talonsteps and dragons shouting. Among the clamor of words, she heard one dragon call to another, "It says the queen is lying!" and someone else yell, "I found another one!" Her messages were getting the attention she'd hoped for — but she'd also hoped she'd be hidden away inside the water tower by now.

Because if the news was spreading through the Hive . . . Wasp only needed to be inside one listening soldier, and then she'd realize Cricket must be here somewhere . . . and then she'd —

Cadelle's eyes flicked over to white, as though all the color had suddenly been leached out of her eyeballs.

"Aha," said the queen of the HiveWings, tipping Cadelle's head toward Cricket. **"There you are."**

CHAPTER 17

Cricket whirled and bolted up the stairs. Behind her, the queen laughed and laughed, an eerie awful cackle that was like something else trying to crawl out through Cadelle's normal laugh.

She made it to the next floor just as three more white-eyed HiveWings burst through the windows, shattering the shutters and ripping down the dark gray curtains. Cricket threw the empty paint pot and paintbrush at them, spattering bright pink droplets everywhere, and hurtled up to the top level, across the guest room and out onto the balcony.

HiveWings were swarming toward Cadelle's house. She could see dragons on every street, running or flying in her direction. The queen had watched Cricket slip through her claws at the Temple of Clearsight; she wasn't going to let her escape again.

Cricket threw herself off the balcony and flew as hard as she could toward the open ledges that led to the savanna. *I escaped the Temple. I can do it again. If I fly and fly . . .*

But this time she didn't have Sundew with her, and the sky was too far away, and there were too many HiveWings, and the queen controlled them all.

They came from everywhere, boiling up from the ground and the windows and the ceilings like an explosion of fire ants. They were tiny dragonets and hulking soldiers and glittering socialites in their jewels and sparkles and finery, but none of them were themselves anymore. They were a swarm; they were the thousand claws of Queen Wasp. They had become mindless weapons.

Cricket had been terrified of the white-eyed dragons ever since that morning when she was two years old. Now she was the dragon they hunted, the dragon who didn't move in unison with everyone else. The dragon who couldn't escape.

She felt talons slam into her back and throw her to the ground. A red-striped HiveWing shot a blast of acid that just missed her shoulder and hissed into the treestuff beside her head. As she tried to roll away, another drove his wrist stingers into the edge of her wings, pinning her to the ground. Cricket shrieked with pain as Cadelle landed on her chest.

Her grandmother did not look triumphant or enraged or even interested. Her face was entirely blank while she held down her granddaughter so a black HiveWing with yellow spots could shoot something painful and paralyzing into Cricket's wings.

Cricket turned her head away from Cadelle's empty face and saw SilkWings watching from the windows and the sidewalks.

Last chance.

Through the haze of pain, she yelled, "The queen is lying to you! The Book never said she should rule you! It was all a lie!" and she thought she saw something — sympathy? confusion? surprise? — flicker in their faces.

And then the yellow-spotted HiveWing shoved his stinger into her neck. Her throat closed over the words she still wanted to say. Her vocal cords radiated with agony and her head flopped over, her neck muscles refusing to work for her anymore.

The HiveWings seized her frozen wings and dragged her away, away from the frightened SilkWing faces and up the ramps, up and up and up to the prison at the center of Lady Jewel's palace.

Every time Cricket thought about the library in Jewel Hive and thought, *Maybe Lady Jewel isn't so bad after all,* she always made herself remember the prison, which Jewel had insisted on building within her own palace walls instead of somewhere a civilized distance away. No one knew why she wanted her prison so close, or what happened to the dragons that disappeared inside it.

I guess I'm about to find out, Cricket thought bleakly as they passed through the blue-and-gold-and-beetle-green silk-spangled gates of Jewel's palace. All the walls inside seemed to be full of windows, so the gray afternoon light and the sound of raindrops and the scent of a storm carried through the entire palace. For a moment, the breeze brushed Cricket's face, whispering of the freedom outside.

And then the HiveWings descended a staircase and Cricket's wings scraped over the black stone threshold that marked the end of Jewel's public palace and the beginning of the secret prison. She wished she could lift her head to see where she was being taken, but all she could do was watch the scuffed floor pass below her, scarred with long trails of desperate claw marks.

Down here there were no windows, and the flamesilk lanterns were few and far between, leaving patches of darkness between dim pools of light. Cricket could hear mournful singing coming from one of the cells as they passed by. Another prisoner called to her — "Hey! What did you do? What did she do? Come on, tell me something!" — but she couldn't answer, and her guards ignored him.

At the end of an interminable corridor, the dragons holding her finally stopped and unlocked a cell. They tossed her inside and she fell face-first, barely catching herself on numb talons before the weight of her paralyzed wings knocked her down. With an enormous effort, she rolled onto her back to see her captors.

"That was easier than I expected," said the queen as one of the HiveWings locked the door. Another HiveWing leaned against the bars, grinning at her. The queen's voice came from both of them at once, which was still immensely creepy. "You really were a fool to come back into a Hive. And for what? A little bit of graffiti, a few pamphlets that will be ash by evening? Poor naïve little dragonet. As though anyone would believe you over their queen."

Cricket couldn't speak; she wasn't sure she would have been able to even if her throat hadn't been paralyzed. She'd never been so scared in her entire life, except maybe the moment when the queen had seen her through the Librarian's eyes, and she'd realized her secret was lost forever.

"It must have been so hard for you," the queen went on, making one of the dragons run his claws along the bars. "Feeling so different, so alone. Watching everyone else come together in my Hive mind, but always left out." The two HiveWings leaned closer and pressed their faces to the bars, as though she might force them to squeeze through. "But I have good news for you, little dragon.

You don't have to be different anymore." Their tongues flickered out and in and out in terrifying unison.

"I can fix you," hissed the queen. "I'm on my way right now. And when I get there . . . I can make you just like everybody else. Aren't you lucky?"

The HiveWings stepped back, their pale eyes still fixed on Cricket. She felt a tear run down her face and couldn't do anything to stop it.

"See you soon, little problem dragon."

The sound of their tails slithering away seemed to last forever as Cricket lay there, alone in the near dark.

Sundew and Blue weren't expecting her until sunset. They wouldn't even look for her until after the queen had already come and done . . . whatever she was going to do.

No one is coming to rescue me. They'll never find me in time.

The queen is going to take my mind and make it hers.

Cricket covered her ears and closed her eyes and prayed to the only dragon who could possibly hear her.

Clearsight, please be listening. Please. Please save me.

CHAPTER 18

When Cricket opened her eyes again, a long time later — almost midday, she sensed — there was an entirely new dragon standing outside the door of her cell, looking in with thoughtful curiosity. Seated next to her, with an enormously grumpy expression, was Lady Scarab.

The new dragon was tall and angular and her scales were a bright golden color that almost looked green in the low flamesilk light. Thin lines of black scales outlined her iridescent green eyes and dotted her cheekbones; more black lines traced the veins in her wings. Gold earrings shaped like beetles hung from her ears, a necklace of onyx stingers rested on her collarbone, and her claws were each painted with perfect lines of black and gold.

Cricket had only seen her once before, across a crowded ballroom, but it was not hard to guess that this was Lady Jewel, ruler of Jewel Hive, daughter of Lady Scarab, and cousin to Queen Wasp. The way she held herself was all regal elegance, as if she were being painted. The only crack in her façade was that she winced a little every time her mother moved, and she seemed to be keeping half an eye on Lady Scarab at all times.

"Hmmm," said Lady Jewel. "So this is the dragon who's thrown my Hive into such a tizzy." She tapped her chin with one long, glittering claw. "You're quite small to cause so much trouble."

"Small and brainless!" Scarab snapped.

"Mother," Jewel said in a warning tone. "You promised you'd be quiet."

Scarab growled.

Cricket tried to sit up and discovered that the paralysis had worn off her wings and neck, although they still ached and she had to move slowly.

"Lady Jewel," she said in a creaky voice.

"No need to bow," Jewel said, waving her talons.

Cricket settled back gratefully. Standing would have been a challenge, to say the least.

"What are you going to do to me?" she whispered.

"That's a fine question to ask NOW!" Scarab bellowed.

"Mother," Jewel said, giving her a quelling look. Scarab glared at both of them and subsided, muttering. Jewel smiled back at Cricket.

"You mean, the torture, the experiments, the vanishing prisoners?" Jewel sat down, coiling her long shining tail around her legs. "Not for you. The queen wants to handle you herself." She shrugged with a faintly disappointed look.

"But if they *were* real, I would say you deserve them!" Scarab interjected.

"MOTHER," Jewel barked as a prisoner a few doors down called, "Eh? Not real? What's that?"

Jewel did something carefully to her face, like smoothing away the cross expression and replacing it with everlasting patience.

"My mother," she said to Cricket, "is not normally allowed in my palace, for reasons that become clearer each time she does visit. She has no idea what I actually do with dragons in my prison."

"Right," snorted Lady Scarab. "I'm sure my daughter who once hid all my knives because they scared her has grown up to become a master torturer."

"What? Really?" called the nosy prisoner.

"Faints at the sight of blood, this one," Scarab added, jerking her head at her daughter.

"I was *five* —" Lady Jewel closed her eyes and took a deep, calming breath. "Let's talk about you," she said, opening them again and looking at Cricket. "Do you know how hard it is to get paint out of treestuff? I'm going to have pink smudges all over my Hive forever now."

"*And* you lost my best paintbrush, didn't you?" Scarab said, lashing her tail.

"Not that my mother had anything to do with this," Jewel added quickly.

"Should have given you an old one," Scarab growled. "But you weren't supposed to get caught, you idiot."

"Oh my gosh, Mom, seriously!" Jewel flapped her wings, the royal stance entirely collapsing. "I am TRYING to be MENACING AND MYSTERIOUS. Could you be quiet for ONE SECOND while I handle this?"

"With what, a new necklace and a party?" Scarab grumbled.

"You may not have noticed, but somehow I manage to be a VERY GOOD HIVE RULER even — I would say *especially* — when you and your advice are on the other side of the continent!"

"Hmm," Scarab said disapprovingly. "The Glitterbazaar would be better if you'd listened to me."

"The Glitterbazaar is FINE!"

"And your schools have absolutely rubbish history programs."

"That's not up to me! Queen Wasp sets the curriculums!

Why do you think I have a giant library full of history books for my subjects?"

"And that table in the front hall is still in the wrong place," Scarab went on. "It would be much more useful as a sideboard in the dining room."

Jewel pressed her claws to her forehead. "Mother," she said, "maybe you should go visit with your grandchildren."

"Not on your life," Scarab said promptly. "Those brats are very loud and I will not be tricked into dragonet-sitting. Stop distracting me and get on with interrogating this nitwit."

"That's what I am TRYING TO —" Jewel stopped and took another deep breath. She turned toward Cricket with a resolutely serene expression. "You. Cricket, right?"

"Yes, that's me," Cricket said. "Did you read my messages? I'm telling the truth. Queen Wasp is lying about the Book of Clearsight."

"I've always suspected that," Jewel said. "Some of our great-great-great-great-grandmothers were not as quick and clever with their lies as Wasp has been. There were hints in the history books, if anyone looked carefully."

"The books?"

"I do read." Jewel smiled, more or less, a tiny quirk of her mouth. "Despite the rumors to the contrary. I'd be quite interested to read the Book of Clearsight."

"I don't have it," Cricket confessed.

"Left it with someone smart enough not to get caught, I hope," Scarab chimed in again. "She says there's no line of HiveWing succession in there, sparkles. You know what that means?"

"That you could have been queen," Jewel said with a sigh.

"That *you* could *still* be queen," Scarab said fiercely. "With my help, of course, or else you'd probably do it all wrong. Paint all the Hives rainbow colors or something."

"Oh, for the — Mother! You can't say things like that!" Jewel leaned back to check up and down the corridor.

"The guards are all the way back at the entrance," Scarab said, flipping her tail from side to side. "They can't hear us."

"I can!" called the prisoner.

"You're a SilkWing," Scarab called back.

"True," he answered. "True."

"Lady Jewel," Cricket said hesitantly. "May I ask — is my sister all right?" She caught herself, remembering. It still felt too strange to call Katydid her mother. "Katydid? She was brought in last night, before me."

"She'll be fine," Jewel said with surprising gentleness. "The queen is less interested in her, now that we have you. I will find out what she knows, which I assume is nothing, and release her before Wasp arrives."

"And that will be when?" Scarab demanded.

"Very soon," Jewel answered. "Which, thank you so much for that; I was supposed to have another three days to prepare before her usual Nest visit."

"She . . . she said she's coming to 'fix' me," Cricket said. "To make me like everyone else. Can she do that?"

Jewel glanced at her mother, pausing for a moment. "Yes. She's done it before."

"What?" Lady Scarab spat. "You never told me that."

"It doesn't always work," Jewel said. "And I don't know how she does it. But we had a pair of dragons in here a few years ago who'd been preparing a case for flamesilk rights. They were pretty old — nearly as old as you, Mother."

"So perhaps not total idiots, then," Scarab snapped.

"Sure," Jewel said. "They said they remembered a time when flamesilks were treated like normal members of the community, selling their flamesilk and living like anyone else. Anyway, Wasp didn't like that very much, so she made my guards drag them in, and she came by and took them into a closed room for a while, and when they came back out, their eyes were white. And they never argued against the queen again."

"I take it back," Scarab huffed. "Total idiots after all. So every time she threatens to add you to her Hive mind . . ."

"She might actually be able to," Jewel said.

"But you don't know how?" Cricket said. "Or what she does to them?"

Jewel shook her head. "I know it doesn't work if they have SilkWing ancestors in the last three generations, though. She keeps all those old dragons penned up together in Tsetse Hive."

"You didn't tell me that, either!" Scarab barked.

"Of course I didn't!" Jewel said, flicking her wings at her mother. "I was afraid you'd go over there and storm around with a protest sign and get yourself thrown in with them!"

"Too right," said Scarab. "Someone needs to give my niece a good thumping."

"Well, I would like you to stay in control of your own brain, as annoying as that brain is, Mother. So I would appreciate it if you could *not* go thumping the queen of our tribe anytime soon."

"If *someone* doesn't thump her soon, we won't have any dragons left who can!" Scarab growled softly to herself and paced off down the corridor.

Cricket tried to stretch the pain out of her wings and neck as she thought. The queen could do something to dragons behind closed doors to make them part of her Hive mind. But surely she hadn't gone to every dragon in every Hive to do it, one at a time, thousands of dragons over fifty years. For one thing, dragons would remember that happening, so everyone would know how she did it — Katydid would have remembered, surely. And dragons would slip through the cracks, and Queen Wasp just couldn't possibly have time to get to every HiveWing that way.

Wait . . .

"Lady Jewel," Cricket said. "Did you say something about the queen coming for a . . . Nest visit?"

"Yes." Jewel tipped her head, studying Cricket. "She visits the Hive Nests twice a year — once in the dry season, once in the rainy season. To ensure that they're clean and safe and full of eggs, according to her rules."

"Do you go into the Nest with her?" Cricket asked.

"No. She always goes alone." Jewel tapped her claws on the floor. "Hmmm."

Scarab reappeared at the bars. "I'm sensing the development of another completely stupid plan."

Cricket got herself to stand and stepped toward the leader of the Hive. "Lady Jewel," she said. "Please let me out of here, and I promise I'll find out what she does in the Nests. If I'm right, and it has something to do with the mind control, maybe we can figure out a way to stop her."

"I can't let you out, little dragonet," Jewel said. "As much as I might be tempted to. Queen Wasp would punish my guards most severely, and they are loyal to me when their minds are their own. They don't deserve that."

"So put those two you don't like on duty," Scarab suggested. "The oily ones who are probably spying on you for the queen."

Jewel narrowed her eyes at her mother for a long moment. "Hmm," she said at length. "That might actually work."

"SEE?" Scarab said triumphantly. "I am full of good advice if you actually listen!"

"By the Book, Mother, I listen to you all the time!"

"Not about those dragonets of yours, you don't. Oof, they are a disaster."

"THEY ARE N — this is not productive." Jewel closed her eyes and rubbed her temples for a moment. "You can only control yourself, you can only control yourself," she murmured. "All right. Let's say I do put those sneaks on guard duty. How would we get her past them?"

Cricket glanced around her cell. "Could I go out another way, instead of through the prison gate? Up or down, maybe?" She scratched the treestuff below her.

"Down would drop you into Rootworm's ballroom, and she would *not* be pleased about that." Lady Jewel looked up at the ceiling, her eyes darting around as though she was measuring the space in her head. "Up . . . I think you'd end up in my kitchens, or close to them. I don't *really* want a hole in my kitchen floor that looks down into a prison cell, but I suppose there are dragons up there who could help you get out of the palace." She tapped her claws again.

"How can I make a hole in treestuff?" Cricket said thoughtfully. "A hammer or something heavy would do it, but it would take a while and the noise would bring the guards." She studied the walls, the bars, the corridor outside . . . "Flamesilk. Flamesilk might work."

"Or it might burn down my palace," Jewel pointed out.

"I'd be careful," Cricket promised.

"And," Scarab observed with unusual cheerfulness, "then Wasp would think her flamesilk friend broke in to get her out. Can't hardly blame you for that, after she lost them twice in her own Hive."

"I suspect Wasp can find a way to blame me no matter what," Jewel said.

"Isn't this why you act like such a vapid banana slug around her?" Scarab asked, flapping her wings. "So she'll think you're a harmless idiot and leave you in peace?"

"I do not!" Jewel protested.

"Ah," said Scarab. "So you actually *are* a harmless idiot?"

Jewel shot her mother a cross look. "The point is, yes, Wasp would not be at all surprised if I lost a dragon from my prisons because she thinks I have nothing but pollen between my ears. That doesn't mean she won't be furious and perfectly nasty to me."

"Perfectly nasty is Wasp's natural resting state," Scarab observed. "You'll survive it. I say it's worth it to keep one more HiveWing free." She nodded at Cricket. "Sneaking into the Nest and spying on the queen, on the other talon, sounds like the height of stupid."

"That's the deal," Jewel said firmly. "I want to follow this theory — and I can't do it myself; she'll have eyes on me."

"I want to know the truth, too," Cricket said, wrapping her talons around the bars. "It's all right, Lady Scarab. I want to do this. I think we'll find answers in there, I really do."

Scarab looked from her daughter to Cricket and back, then flung her wings up with a snort. "Fine. Let's get this daft dragonet some flamesilk."

— CHAPTER 19 —

Cricket waited, as she'd been instructed, until Lady Jewel and Scarab were long gone — long enough for Jewel to have replaced the guards at the front entrance of the prison. Then she took out the little stone pot of flamesilk that Jewel had left with her. The golden thread inside glowed bright and hot; she guessed it was very new.

Maybe it's even Blue's, she thought. *Maybe one of the dragons in the market traded it up through the Hive yesterday, so it wound up here in Jewel's palace.*

She liked that thought, that maybe a little piece of Blue was going to help her escape.

She still had the flamesilk tweezers she'd taken from her school library the night she ran away with Blue. Carefully she used them to twist the thread of flamesilk until it was straight and taut like a wire, and then she lifted the thread out and flew up to the ceiling.

It was very awkward, trying to keep herself in the air nearly upside down and work on the ceiling without dropping the flamesilk thread. She traced out a circle big enough for her to fit through, leaving a black smoking line with small flickers of flame curling from a few of the edges. Then she traced it again, and again, pressing the flamesilk farther into the treestuff.

She knew treestuff was made of bits of wood pulp, silk, and clay, and she guessed that how quickly it burned would depend on how much of each was in this section of the ceiling. Tracing the line seemed to take forever, around and around, over and over again. Her wings started to ache and she had to land back on the floor for a little while to rest them.

"Pssst," called a voice from the hallway. Cricket edged over to the bars and tried to peer out. She could see light purple talons waving from a cell a few doors away.

"Yes?" she whispered back.

"I didn't catch all that," said the prisoner, "but if I want to stay on Lady Jewel's good side — and I fervently do — what should I say to the queen when she asks me how you escaped?"

Cricket was silent for a moment, worrying. "Why wouldn't you tell the queen what you heard?" she asked.

"Because Lady Jewel is the only ruler in the Hives who can be trusted," the SilkWing whispered back. "Queen Wasp has no sense of mercy or justice. I'm due to be released tomorrow, and I think Lady Jewel will be fair with me."

"I think so, too," Cricket said, wondering now about the stories of Jewel's prison. What if the dragons who disappeared in here were actually spirited away to safety by Jewel, to keep them out of the queen's talons? She let the queen and everyone else think that cruel, secretive things went on behind the prison doors, but perhaps that was a clever way to conceal what she really did for dragons in trouble.

"What are you in here for?" Cricket asked.

"Not paying my library fines," the dragon answered ruefully.

Cricket wished he could see her smile. "If you could tell the queen," she said, "that you think you heard a dragon burn a hole in my ceiling from the other side, that would be very helpful."

"I could do that," he said. "And when you saw this dragon, you shouted . . ."

"Blue," Cricket said. "She'll expect it was him."

"Good luck," the prisoner said, waving his talons through the bars again.

Cricket returned to the scorched line in the ceiling, burning it again and again. She didn't know how long it took to fly from Wasp Hive to Jewel Hive, but she felt the queen drawing closer with every heartbeat. She had to hurry.

Finally she felt the thread break through into open space on the other side of the ceiling. The circle of treestuff trembled above her, barely hanging in place, and she shoved it hard with her shoulder.

"Stand back," someone called from above.

Startled, Cricket flew to the side. She heard a thump, and then another, and then the circle fell out of the ceiling in a crash of treestuff dust.

"That'll bring the guards," the other prisoner called. "Better hurry and go."

"Come on," cried the voice from the next level up. Cricket saw dark orange claws beckoning through the hole in the ceiling. She darted over and squeezed herself through, folding her wings in as tight as they'd go and losing a few scarves in the process. Talons reached for her, tugging her upward until she tumbled free onto the floor of Jewel's palace kitchen.

Five SilkWing servants were scattered around the room, staring at her with wide eyes, frozen in the middle of chopping or stirring or roasting or whatever they'd been doing. But standing by the hole were Cinnabar and Tau, the

SilkWings from the Chrysalis. They were the ones who'd helped her climb through.

"You're all right," Cricket gasped. "I thought Lady Jewel was going to punish you."

"Not much," Tau said. "She likes me."

"She likes me, too!" Cinnabar huffed, taking the stone jar from Cricket. Cricket dropped the flamesilk into it, and Cinnabar neatly capped the jar and slotted it onto a high shelf between glass jars labeled BASIL and GINGER.

"Not as much as she likes me," Tau said serenely. "Also, whenever the queen says to punish us severely, Jewel gives us a medal." She clapped at a few of the watching SilkWings. "Pour some water over this hole to make sure it doesn't burn further. And you were all in the pantry and saw nothing."

"Yes, Tau," one of them answered. The others bowed their heads in agreement.

"Follow us," Cinnabar said to Cricket, turning and sprinting out of the kitchen. Cricket followed, with Tau at her side.

They ran through the winding back passages of the palace, narrow halls that Cricket guessed were intended for servants, to keep them out of sight of Jewel's HiveWing guests. She caught glimpses of jewel-toned ballrooms as they flew by, ruby-red walls and yellow silk banners and emerald patterns in the floors. She could still hear the rain and feel the breeze from outside in almost every room.

At last they came to a small, nondescript door. Cinnabar opened it and peeked outside; a gust of wind came through, carrying the savanna scents of sunlight and rain and grass. She closed it again quickly and looked back at Tau.

"Treehopper is out there," she said softly.

Cricket wondered if Blue could have read Tau's expression, because she couldn't at all. The gentle SilkWing was either smothering a smile or trying not to bite something.

"Is he . . . himself?" she asked.

"I couldn't tell," Cinnabar said. "His back is to the door."

"I'll talk to him." Tau stepped forward, brushing past Cricket in the dim hallway.

"Is that a good idea?" Cinnabar asked. "With the queen so close?"

"I am Lady Jewel's chief steward," Tau said austerely, "and he is her treasurer. We are allowed to have an ordinary, everyday conversation."

Cinnabar quirked an eyebrow at her.

"I promise we won't be obvious," Tau said in her normal voice. "Really, Cinnabar."

"You're obvious every time you even *look* at each other," Cinnabar grumbled. "Just get away from him quick if his eyes go white."

Tau shuddered. "I always do."

She slipped out through the door and Cricket nudged up to peek through the crack with Cinnabar.

Outside, a wide balcony garden overlooked the savanna, covered in plants of all shapes and sizes. Raspberry bushes lined the paths and white honeysuckle climbed the gazebos. Cricket spotted pale pink lotus flowers drifting across the ponds and clusters of forget-me-nots everywhere. The way most of the plants spilled over their borders made her miss her little terrarium back at school, even though she'd always found the endless botany classes rather boring.

It was raining, a quiet, gentle rainfall, but a roof extended over part of the gardens, and underneath it, a plump, worried-looking HiveWing sat by one of the pools, reading. His scales were a dark greenish black with pale orange stripes along his wings, tail, and face. He turned to look up as Tau approached and Cricket saw what Cinnabar meant: his whole face lit up as though he'd just discovered sunshine.

"By the Hive," Cinnabar muttered. "They're terrible at this."

"He's a HiveWing," Cricket whispered. "And she's a SilkWing."

"Yup," said Cinnabar. "Extra very forbidden. It's a problem, and we all know it, even Lady Jewel, but no one can do anything about it."

Seeing the two dragons laughing, their wings brushing accidentally, Cricket knew she wouldn't have been able to do anything about it, either. Even if she were their queen, she'd never be able to separate two dragons who looked so happy together.

"All right, stop being cute and get him out of there," Cinnabar grumbled between her teeth.

Tau gestured toward a door on the other side of the garden, and they both started walking in that direction. Cinnabar poked her nose out a little farther, watching them go.

And then Treehopper froze in place for a moment. Tau stumbled beside him, glanced at him quickly, and ducked her head, her whole posture changing instantly into that of a dutiful servant.

The HiveWing turned his head in a slow, eerie twist to scan the garden. Cricket and Cinnabar jumped back behind the door before the white eyes got to them.

"I have arrived," said the queen's chilly voice. Cricket felt a spasm of fear shoot through her from snout to tail. "Jewel. Meet me in the prison."

There was a pause, and then Treehopper shook himself with a hiss. "Sorry," he said in a low voice to Tau, looking down at his talons as though he couldn't bear to meet her eyes.

"It's not your fault," she said softly.

Cricket's heart was thundering in her ears. She was sure she could hear talonsteps coming along the corridor; any moment the queen would step into the prison and see her empty cell. Unless she knew already . . . maybe she'd seen it through her spies. Any moment the queen would take over the entire Hive again and Cricket would be surrounded by her.

The two dragons in the garden went through the far door at last. Cinnabar and Cricket leaped out of their hiding spot and ran for the edge.

"If you were smart," Cinnabar said, "you'd fly out that way and never stop." She pointed out at the ocean beyond Dragonfly Bay.

I wish I could. Cricket thought of her dream of the Distant Kingdoms, where Clearsight had come from. She and Blue could be safe over there, out of reach of Queen Wasp's claws.

"I promised Lady Jewel I'd find some answers for her first," she told Cinnabar. "Thank you for your help."

The dark orange dragon waved as Cricket dove into the air and twisted her wings to spiral down the side of the Hive. Other dragons were out despite the rain, flitting from one ledge to another or venturing into the wet savanna for prey. She wove through them, keeping an eye on the HiveWings, until she found an open ledge on the Nest level and could duck inside.

The walkways around the Nest were little pebbled paths dotted with benches where dragons could meet and make plans for their future offspring. The paths circled the giant dome, which was painted smooth and white like an eggshell. Cricket had visited the Cicada Hive Nest once, and it looked a lot like this. She'd seen parents meeting with administrators to decide what schools their dragonets would attend; she'd even seen some discussing arranged marriage plans.

But the walkways around the Jewel Hive Nest were empty. She crept up to the snowy walls of the dome and around to the main door, which was opposite the entrance to the ramps. A sign was posted on the door of the dome: CLOSED FOR INSPECTION BY THE QUEEN.

Oh, moons, Cricket thought. *Please don't be in there already.* She glanced around and spotted two guards pacing up and down the ramps. Quickly she dove behind a bench and peered at them through the slats.

Their attention was focused outward, steering dragons away from the Nest. They didn't look back at the dome. They could, any second . . . but while she was watching, they didn't, and she had to hope she'd be lucky.

Taking a deep breath, she darted to the door, pulled it open, and ducked inside. It swung shut behind her and she caught it with her tail so it wouldn't thud.

The inside of the dome was very dark. For a moment, Cricket was afraid that there was no light in there at all, and for a moment, with a shiver of fear, she wondered whether Queen Wasp could see in the dark.

She could be in here, watching me, right now.

Cricket stood petrified by the door, trying to breathe quietly, and slowly she realized that her eyes were adjusting, and the Nest was not completely dark after all.

It was not lit by flamesilk, though. The glowing green light came from small clouds of bioluminescent mushrooms gathered in clumps all around the room, at the base of the walls, and along the paths between the eggs. There was something weird and haunted and beautiful about the scene, as though Cricket had wandered onto the surface of one of the moons.

The Nest was full of eggs, cradled in small hollows in the floor, ten apiece. Cricket shivered again, thinking of all the tiny heartbeats under the shells, all the little dragons waiting to hatch. She stepped onto one of the paths and studied the closest egg.

A name was written on the shell in ink — the mother's name, Cricket guessed. And below that, scored into the shell, there was something else, some kind of symbol. Cricket bent closer. It looked like a pair of stingers, arcing sharply away from each other like the antennae of a wasp.

She checked the next egg, and the next. They all bore the same marking, until she came around to a group of newer eggs. These had only half the marking: one sharp line, traced ominously along the curve of the shells.

The very newest ones had no marks on them at all.

Cricket's mind was buzzing with questions, but she knew she'd already spent too long gazing at the eggs. She needed to find a place to hide, which would be nearly impossible in a room that contained nothing but eggs and glowing toadstools.

She turned, searching the shadows, and her tail bumped one of the larger eggs in the last hollow. It rocked slightly in its crevice and she jumped forward to catch it. She could feel the vibrations of the dragonet moving under the shell.

This egg had only one mark on it. And instead of a name, the word written on the shell was ORPHANAGE.

Poor little dragonet, Cricket thought. *He or she won't even have a Katydid. Yesterday I thought for a while that I'd never known my parents — but this one really never will. And Queen Wasp will be able to control this dragonet whenever she wants; they'll never have a chance to be free.*

A strange instinct seized her, and she wrapped the egg in one of her scarves, tying it to her chest. Then she looked up, blinking back tears, and saw the rafters.

The Nest was not a perfect dome; it had cracked and shifted over the years since it was built. Four tall columns and a pair of crossbeams had been added at some point to keep the structure stable.

Up there, in the shadow where the support beams met . . . maybe she could hide up there.

Cricket spread her wings and flew up to the crossbeams. She crept cautiously along them, finally settling in what seemed to be the darkest corner, right above the door.

She might kill me for this. Cricket didn't know where the line of treason was for the queen. Would she be content to take Cricket's brain and freedom from her? Or would spying on her secrets mean certain death? If so, knowing about the Book was cause enough to kill her, surely.

I think it's safe to say that if the queen catches me, I'm in enormous trouble no matter what she decides to do.

Cricket wrapped her wings around the egg and curled into the smallest ball she could make. She thought about Blue and Sundew and Swordtail, hiding somewhere. There was still time before sunset. If the answer to the mind-control question was here . . . she had to hope Sundew could get the message to her parents before they did something terrible and irreversible.

But sunset crept closer and closer, and nobody came into the dome.

Cricket began to worry that the queen wasn't coming. What if she was so furious about Cricket escaping that she'd decided to skip the Nest visit in favor of taking over the whole tribe to search for her? Or what if she was busy punishing the dragons in Jewel's palace for letting Cricket escape?

I hope Lady Jewel is all right. And Cinnabar and Tau. And Lady Scarab.

She hoped Jewel had had time to free Katydid, as she'd promised, before the queen arrived.

She could feel the sun sinking down the sky, and she was beginning to imagine the most terrible scenes happening back at the palace, when suddenly she heard a soft creak, and a bar of light lanced across the eggs.

It was Queen Wasp, at last.

CHAPTER 20

The queen stalked forward into the Nest on soundless talons. The door snicked shut behind her, and Cricket watched the queen pause, surveying the eggs.

Or letting her eyes adjust, Cricket thought. *Maybe she can't see in the dark after all.*

That thought did not make the queen any less terrifying. Queen Wasp was enormous, even from Cricket's vantage point, up by the dome's ceiling. Cricket knew, logically, that Wasp was probably smaller than Lady Scarab, as Scarab was older than her. But there was something about the way Queen Wasp stood and held her wings and radiated menace that made her seem quite possibly the largest dragon in the entire world.

Her name was well-chosen, too. From above, Cricket had a perfect view of the yellow and black stripes and black horns that made the queen look so much like one of the Pantalan wasps that could kill an elephant with its venom.

Cricket breathed as lightly, softly as she could, trying not to move or shift or twitch.

The queen stepped between the eggs, her head twisting abruptly to one side, then to the other, her tongue flicking in and out. She passed the hollows of eggs with the double marks. Her tail slid behind her like a cobra stalking its prey.

She reached the first group of newer eggs, those with only one stinger marked on them. Here she stopped, hissing for a long, terrifying moment.

Queen Wasp picked up one of the eggs. Her tail rose behind her and a long, needle-sharp stinger slid out of the tip.

Cricket fought back a gasp. Everyone knew about the stingers in Queen Wasp's claws, and how much pain they could inject. She'd never heard anyone mention a stinger in the queen's tail as well.

In a move like a flash of lightning, the queen struck, plunging her tail stinger into the eggshell. A pulse of something bright green seemed to move through the stinger into the egg — *into the dragonet inside*, Cricket thought with mute horror — and then the queen drew her stinger out and dropped the egg back into place. With one claw, she sketched the second half of the marking on the shell, and then she picked up the next egg.

Cricket could only watch a few more before she had to close her eyes and bury her face in the egg she held. The queen moved quickly, efficiently, ruthlessly. And Cricket knew what she was seeing.

This is how she does it. She poisons her dragons before they've even hatched. They come into the world already linked to her by whatever that is she's injecting into the eggs. The moment they open their eyes, she can be there, inside their heads.

Does it take two injections to work? Or is one for backup? She glanced down at the orphaned egg she was cradling in the scarf. Would this dragon belong to the queen already, or could it be free if the queen never stabbed it a second time?

I came from a Nest, too. So why not me?

She thought for a while, trying to ignore the soft chilling noises from below her.

Scarab said Katydid was trying to hide my egg at first. She smuggled me into a Nest later, after I'd been an egg for a while.

She must have seen the marks, too, and not known what they meant.

I bet she marked my egg herself. So later the queen thought she'd already stabbed me.

That's how I escaped.

She brushed her talons gently over the single mark on the egg. Which marking had Katydid put on the egg? Maybe Cricket had been injected, but only once instead of twice. She tightened her grip on the scarf. It was nauseating to think of the queen plunging her poison into Cricket — still worse to know she was doing it now to all these baby dragons.

I wish I could stop her. I wish I could fly down there and drop a deadly centipede on her head or drown her in flamesilk. I wish I were brave or fierce or dangerous.

But she couldn't do anything . . . not here, not now. She had only one weapon: she knew the truth about the queen. And right now, she was the only one who knew. She had to stay safe to make sure she could get that information to Lady Jewel, and maybe to the whole tribe, if she could.

So she stayed in the rafters, as still as a mouse with hawks overhead, while the queen finished her gruesome work. The last egg was set down, the last shell marked, and Queen Wasp slithered out the door as silently as she'd arrived.

Cricket checked her internal sense of time and felt a spasm of panic. It was almost sunset. She wanted to leap off her perch and race down to the Glitterbazaar, but she needed to wait long enough for the queen to be definitely gone.

Now? Now? Is it safe? Can I go now?

She wondered if something about her humming anxiety translated through the eggshell in her arms, because she felt the dragonet inside move again, rolling and scrunching around.

Finally she'd waited as long as she could and she flew back down to the ground. She glanced around at the eggs, feeling her wings droop to either side of her.

"I'm sorry, little dragons," she whispered. "I wish I could save you all."

Cricket pressed her ear to the door and listened for a long time but heard nothing outside. Pulling her scarves closer, she opened the door a crack and peeked out.

The guards were gone. She could see dragons moving up and down the ramps, but she couldn't tell if they were mind-controlled or not. It felt horribly likely that the queen would have the whole Hive on alert, looking for her.

She slipped out and around the curve of the dome, back toward the sky ledge. It would be safer to fly than to try creeping down all the levels inside the Hive, past the hundreds of eyes that could be looking for her.

Or perhaps not. Cricket hesitated on the ledge. The light drizzle from earlier had strengthened into a driving storm. Rain poured down with a vengeance, lightning crackled on the horizon, and the wind was strong enough to shake the Hive. Even standing inside the Hive, Cricket felt the spray of raindrops on her face, as though the entire sea was throwing itself around in fury.

Still safer than the zombie eyes, Cricket told herself. She didn't want to get caught again. She *would not* get caught again, especially with this egg — and a dragonet inside who had a chance to be free, like her.

She took a deep breath and plunged into the storm. The wind howled furiously and tried to smash her against the Hive walls, but she folded her wings and dropped, plummeting toward the earth. Rain battered her face, nearly blinding her, but she managed to pull up just before she hit the outer Glitterbazaar canopy. Below it, she could see the shapes of dragons rushing to fix the leaks and protect their wares.

Her scarves felt like wet seaweed, clinging to her neck and legs. She landed in a mud puddle outside the market and squelched toward the end of the stalls. The egg vibrated in its soaking-wet makeshift sling, nearly slipping away from her a couple of times.

She had her head down and eyes nearly closed against the downpour, so when a dragon ducked under the canopy and stepped in front of her, she almost ran straight into him.

"Cricket!" he yelled over the rush of the wind.

"Blue!" she cried joyfully. "You're all right!"

"*You're* all right!" he shouted back, beaming. He swept her up in his wings, azure warmth surrounding her as she felt safe for the first time all day. "I worried about you so much."

"Any luck searching for Luna?" she asked.

"No," he said into her shoulder with a sigh. "Sundew thinks we should ask the LeafWings if they've seen her. Whoa . . . why do you have an egg with you?"

"I saved it from the queen," Cricket said, pulling back a little so he could see the smooth white shell. "Where's Sundew? Has she sent a message to the other LeafWings yet?"

"I don't think so." They both glanced up at the dark clouds overhead. Raindrops cascaded down Blue's face like tiny sapphires. It was impossible to see the sun, but Cricket knew it was sinking.

Am I too late? What are the LeafWings planning? Can I still stop them?

"I have to talk to her, quickly," Cricket said.

"This way." Blue guided her to the canopy and lifted an edge so she could slide underneath.

Cricket found herself in a small, rickety-looking stall with rain dripping through a tear in the web overhead. A SilkWing was hovering by the hole, trying to patch it with his silk. Swordtail was up there, too, helping to hold it together.

She couldn't identify right away what was for sale in here — the shelves seemed to hold a mishmash of items, from little pots of blackberries to damp silk pillows, a few cracked mirrors, a very unfortunate-smelling pile of wildebeest pelts, and a barrel labeled SEEDS. There was not much room to maneuver between the tent walls. Cricket felt oversized and wet and very muddy. She started unwinding all the wet scarves around her.

Tau appeared from under one of the tables. "I can't believe you made it here," she said. "The queen is *livid*. Everyone in the Hive is supposed to be looking for you." She followed Cricket's glance up to the SilkWing on the ceiling. "That's my stepbrother; don't worry, he's in the Chrysalis. We can trust him."

"Is Lady Jewel all right?" Cricket asked.

"She will be, I think. She's made the queen this mad before and survived, mostly because the queen thinks she's a butterfly-brain who could never execute an actual plan."

"Can you take her a message for me? I found out what the queen is doing in the Nest — but I have to tell Sundew first."

"I'm here," Sundew said, pushing her way through a curtain from the next room. Her SilkWing disguise had been abandoned; she looked like herself again. Cricket felt a surge of relief at the sight of her serious green face.

"Sundew!" she cried. "We can tell your parents I know how the queen does it! She's poisoning dragons when they're still in their eggs — I saw her stabbing them with her tail stinger. She goes to every Nest in all the Hives to do it. That way when they hatch she can mind-control them right away. Apparently she can inject grown dragons, too, but it must be faster to do all the eggs at once."

"To grown dragons?" Blue echoed. "You mean . . . could she do it to you?"

Cricket tried not to let it show on her face how scared she'd been, or how close she'd come to that exact fate today. "Yes, I think so," she said. "I think she missed stabbing my egg because Katydid snuck me into the nest late. But if she got her claws on me now, she could force me into the Hive mind."

"*No,*" Blue said passionately. "That is never, *never* going to happen!"

Cricket brushed his wings with hers. "We can save other eggs like I was saved. Sundew, don't you see? What Queen Wasp can do, it's not a power — I mean, it is, but it doesn't have to be — HiveWings could be free. This one *will* be free."

She held out the egg and Sundew touched it lightly, as though she wasn't entirely convinced it was safe to have around.

"Wow," said the LeafWing. "That is . . . a lot of information."

"We have to tell your parents to call off their other plan," Cricket said breathlessly. "It's sunset; we have to do it now. How do we get to them?"

Sundew made a face — her trying-not-to-make-a-face

face. "Cricket . . . it's amazing and insane and creepy what you found, but it doesn't change anything."

"Of course it does!" Cricket pulled the egg back into her chest. "We can stop her from stabbing any more eggs! Once I tell Lady Jewel, I know she'll come up with some way to protect them — maybe the other Hive rulers will, too."

"But even if they can — and I don't see how, with Queen Wasp still in charge — but even if we could save the eggs, we can't save the dragons who are already in her Hive mind, can we?" Sundew asked. "We still have an entire tribe of Wasp-brains to deal with, right? There's no way to shut it down."

Cricket glanced around as Blue wove his tail through hers. "There might be," he said. "Ask your parents for more time — maybe we can find out more."

"They are really not going to like that," Sundew said. "Our dragons want vengeance, HiveWing. The last time I saw my parents, they barely listened to my report at all."

"But nobody wants another war, do they?" Cricket brushed rain and tears off her face. "Don't they remember how terrible the Tree Wars were?"

"Of course they do," said Sundew. "That's exactly why they're doing this. The HiveWings started it. The LeafWings are going to end it."

"It must be awful," Blue said, "thinking that war is the

only solution." He lifted the egg gently out of Cricket's talons and dried it with his cape.

"Isn't there something we can do?" Cricket said again. "There must be something. We know Queen Wasp's secrets now. If we tell everyone . . . if dragons knew the truth . . ."

"They still couldn't stop her," Sundew said. "She controls them completely."

"Not the SilkWings," Tau said. "This information could make a big difference to the Chrysalis. And Lady Jewel."

"You should tell them, then," Sundew said. "But I don't think my parents will care."

"Would they listen to us?" Blue asked. "Could we try talking to them? What if . . . what if I offered to give them some of my flamesilk in exchange for more time? Cricket, maybe we could negotiate with them."

"You don't have to do that," Cricket said, taking one of his talons and brushing her claws over the glowing scales.

"I would, though," Blue said. "I want to stop this war, too. Sundew? Can we please try?"

The LeafWing spread her gold-dappled green wings and sighed. "We can try," she said. "I'll take you to them. They're waiting for me right now."

"Can we also ask them to leave Jewel Hive out of it?" Cricket asked. "For as long as possible, anyway? Lady Jewel would be on your side if you don't hurt her dragons, I really think she would."

"I agree," Tau said.

"We'll ask," Sundew said, looking torn. "But . . . Tau, if you can find a reason to get all the SilkWing dragonets out of the Hive, to somewhere safe . . . that might be a good idea, is all I can say." She looked up at the ceiling. "Swordtail! We're leaving!"

Swordtail hopped down to the ground and gave Cricket a nudge. "Glad you're all right," he said gruffly.

Cricket told Tau everything she'd seen inside the Nest while her friends gathered their things. Tau pressed her talons together, looking worried. "Are you sure that dragonet won't have the queen in its head, too?" she asked, nodding at the egg.

"That's what I want to find out," Cricket said.

"Seems like a risky experiment."

"I am a scientist," Cricket said. "Sometimes risks are necessary." She'd said those words many times in her life, although they had never gotten her out of any of the trouble her experiments had gotten her into. But it felt different now, real and serious.

She wrung out her scarves and wrapped up the egg again, tying it to her even more securely. She guessed they'd be flying all night in a thunderstorm, and she wanted to keep it warm and safe.

The truth was, the dragonet in the egg wasn't just an experiment. It was someone who could be free of the Hive mind — the first dragon she could save from Queen Wasp.

Hopefully the first of many.

If this works. If we get away from here without being caught. If we make it to the LeafWings and convince them to give us more time and find a way to stop the mind control.

If nothing went wrong, this dragonet might have a chance at a better life . . . and all the tribes might have a chance at peace.

CHAPTER 21

Cricket woke up the next morning into a feeling of lingering dread. She had dreamed about losing the orphan egg, about Queen Wasp stabbing her in the heart with her mind-control poison, about Sundew opening her palms and unleashing an army of swarming black insects that covered Pantala from coast to coast.

She opened her eyes and found herself curled tight around the egg. Cool scales rested against her back, and when she peeked over her shoulder, she found Blue asleep with one wing tented over hers.

Sundew had brought them to a peninsula northeast of Jewel Hive, to a cave at the bottom of the seaside cliffs, but when they arrived late the night before, there was no sign of Belladonna or Hemlock. It had still been raining when they crept into the shallow nook and curled up on the damp rocks, but sometime in the night the rain must have stopped. There was no more thunder; the howling wind had finally dozed off. She could see the waters of Dragonfly Bay outside, leaden and gray like the clouds above them.

Carefully Cricket slid herself up to sitting and checked the egg.

There was a crack along the top of the shell.

Her heart stopped, and she touched it gently with one claw, then held the egg up to listen to it. *Is the dragonet all right? Did I crack the egg?*

As soon as she lifted it, a brisk tapping sound came from inside the shell. Something poked at the crack from the other side.

Is it HATCHING?

Cricket knew she shouldn't be quite so alarmed. Hatching was, in fact, what eggs did. This one had to hatch at some point.

But she'd really thought she'd have a few more days first! How could she possibly have grabbed an egg *that* close to hatching? The queen had originally planned to visit three days later — surely she timed her visits to catch all the eggs before their hatching times?

"No," Cricket said firmly to the egg. "It is NOT TIME TO HATCH YET."

The tapping paused, and then picked up speed.

"Stop that!" Cricket said. "What are you doing? You're not ready to hatch! You can't come out!" She put one talon over the crack, covering it up.

The dragonet inside jabbed her palm with one of its claws.

"Stay," Cricket ordered. "Stay IN THERE."

"That sounds like it's going well," Sundew commented from across the cave, opening one bleary eye to glare at her.

"It cannot possibly be time for this egg to hatch," Cricket said.

"I think it disagrees with you," Sundew observed.

Blue sat up, yawning, and looked over Cricket's shoulder. "Maybe it thinks it's time to hatch because it's not in the Nest anymore."

"Oh my stars," Cricket said. "Is that a thing? A real thing? Can it really tell it's not in the Nest?"

"Well, the light is different, and the noises outside the shell, and it's being moved around a lot more — so maybe?" Blue guessed.

"I thought you were the one who knew things," Sundew said to Cricket.

"Not about eggs and dragonets and hatching!" Cricket said. "I've never studied those! I know about seeds and dirt and plants and . . . oh no, Blue, you might be right. Are eggs like seeds? Like if you put them in the right conditions, they grow?"

He spread his wings with an "I have no idea" expression.

"Baby," Cricket said to the egg. "Small dragon. This would be a VERY SILLY place and time to hatch. Do not do it."

A claw poked straight through the crack and wiggled gleefully at her.

Cricket gave Sundew a helpless look.

"This was your brilliant idea," Sundew said. "Don't look at me. I don't want anything to do with any dragonets. Especially a *HiveWing* dragonet." She jumped to her feet. "I'll go get us something to eat. Yes, that's what I should do." She hurried out of the cave, casting the egg a suspicious look as she went by.

"It's going to be very confused," Blue said. "Don't you think? Or maybe not; I guess it probably doesn't have any expectations about what hatching will be like. I wonder if it's scared."

The egg was rocking merrily back and forth, emitting tiny squeaks. "Somehow I think not," Cricket said.

More cracks spidered out from the first one. Delighted with its success, the dragonet kicked harder, finally sending a fragment of eggshell flying off to whap into Cricket's nose.

"I'm serious!" Cricket yelped at it. "Stop hatching right now!"

The eggshell cracked in half in her talons. The pieces fell away, leaving a small black-and-yellow dragonet sitting between her claws, happily shaking bits of eggshell and goop off her wings.

"Whoa." Blue leaned closer and blinked at it.

"Oh *no*," said Cricket.

"Yim!" declared the dragonet, accidentally whacking Blue in the snout with her tail.

"Awwww," Swordtail said from across the cave. "Look how cute she is!"

"Rrrrpt," the dragonet agreed. She seized one of Cricket's claws and started chewing on it.

"No, thank you, OW," Cricket said, tugging her off and lifting her up so they were eye to eye.

"OW," the dragonet mimicked solemnly. "OW." She reached for Cricket's ear with a hungry expression.

"She is cute," Blue said, smiling.

"She is *trying* to *eat me*," Cricket pointed out. "Sundew! I know you can hear me! Did you find any food?"

Sundew poked her head into the cave. "I perhaps should have mentioned this sooner," she said, "but I rather intensely dislike small dragonets."

"GORB," the dragonet said sternly. "OW."

"Here," Sundew said, tossing a fish across the cave to Cricket. Blue jumped forward and caught it for her. "But don't you dare let it think food comes from me!"

Cricket gave the fish to the dragonet and set her down in a small hollow in the rocks. The baby stuck the fish in her mouth, chewed vigorously for a moment, and then keeled over and fell asleep.

"So cute," Swordtail said again, inching closer to grin at her.

"She needs a name," Blue said. They all looked down at her black scales, striped with wide fuzzy swaths of bright yellow.

"She looks kind of like a bumblebee," Cricket said.

"Bumblebee," Swordtail echoed. "I like that."

"Me too," Blue agreed.

"*I* have no opinion," Sundew offered from her spot half-way out the door.

"Come peek at her," Swordtail said. "It's safe while she's sleeping."

"Not interested," Sundew said firmly.

Cricket leaned down and picked up the two halves of the eggshell. The dragonet seemed normal, as far as she could tell, if perhaps a little noisy and hyper and ravenous. Although she really had no idea what a normal dragonet should be like. Bumblebee hadn't gone white-eyed in the twenty heartbeats she'd been awake, anyhow. Cricket wasn't quite sure what the next step of this experiment was. Wait until Queen Wasp *did* look out of her eyes? If that happened, what would they do with Bumblebee? Abandon her somewhere?

I won't ever do that.

But it's not going to happen. She was only injected once. Like me, probably. She'll be free.

Something caught her attention and she squinted at the eggshells for a moment.

"Blue," she said, "do you see this?"

He leaned over and looked. "That's the inside of Bumblebee's shell? It looks kind of . . . greenish."

"Let me see." Sundew crossed the cave and Cricket held the shells up to the light. There was definitely some kind of green residue dusting the inside of the shells.

Sundew took one shell and poked the green part, but it didn't brush off. It looked like a thin green crust, almost baked onto the shell. She frowned at it for a moment, then lifted it to her snout and sniffed it.

"Yuck," Swordtail declared.

"I know this smell," Sundew said. She stared out at the bay for a moment, then sniffed it again.

Cricket sniffed the one she was holding. It had a dark, leaf-rot scent, with something unpleasantly peppery lurking inside it. There was something a little familiar about it, but nothing she could identify.

"I spent four days surrounded by this smell," Sundew said.

"What?" Cricket said, startled. "Where?"

"It comes from a plant," Sundew said. "And Queen Wasp's private greenhouse is full of it."

CHAPTER 22

Cricket gasped. "The greenhouse where we met you?"

"Where we *captured* you," Sundew corrected her.

"The one that says 'Queen Wasp's top secret greenhouse keep out or I will dismember you and then kill you some more'?" Blue asked.

"That's the one," Sundew said. "There were other plants in it, too, but that's the main one. It's *everywhere* in there. And it smells terrible."

"Sundew — is that what she's using?" Cricket asked. "Could a plant give her mind-control powers? Maybe for instance if she ate a lot of it and then injected it into her victims?"

"I don't know!" Sundew snapped. "I've never heard of a plant like that, but I'd call this a clue, don't you think?" She waved the eggshell at them.

"Yeergh," Blue said, wrinkling his snout at the green stuff. "I wonder if it tastes as bad as it smells."

"I certainly hope so," Swordtail said. "I hope she has to eat Hiveloads of it."

"This could be the way to save the dragonets," Cricket said, meeting Sundew's eyes. "Right? Couldn't we destroy her supply? And then she won't be able to eat it or inject it into them. Or do it to any grown-up dragons like Lady Jewel, either."

"Like you," Blue said. He sat up with an alert expression. "Then *you'd* be safe from her. Let's do it."

"You had me at 'destroy,'" Swordtail offered.

"I'm up for it," Sundew said, spreading her wings, "but it's not that easy. Wasp Hive is swarming with soldiers since we stole the Book of Clearsight and broke into the flamesilk cavern. There are guards patrolling the greenhouses all the time. Queen Wasp is in their heads more than half the day, keeping watch. I don't see how we'll get anywhere near it without getting caught."

They sat in silence for a moment. Cricket's mind was spinning through possibilities. If this was the answer . . . if they could take the queen's power away . . . it was a start, at least. It might not stop the LeafWings' plans for war, but it would give the next generation a chance against Queen Wasp . . . if they survived that war.

"We'll tell my parents," Sundew said. "Belladonna will know what to do with this information. Maybe they can take a pod of LeafWings to attack the greenhouse."

"A what?" Cricket asked.

"A pod," Sundew repeated. "Like, a small group, part of the warrior force."

"Are you part of the warrior force?" Swordtail asked.

Sundew made one of her inscrutable faces. "Sort of. I'm . . . kind of my own pod."

"Where are your parents?" Cricket asked. "Why aren't they here?" She glanced over to make sure that Bumblebee was still sleeping and saw that she'd flopped over on her back with the fish still hanging out of her mouth. Tiny snores emitted from her snout.

"I don't know. They should be." Sundew went back to the mouth of the cave, looking out at the bay. "I hope nothing went wrong," she said quietly.

"Um . . . what's that?" Blue asked, pointing south across the water. Cricket joined them on the edge of the rocks, followed by Swordtail. All four dragons squinted out into the gray morning.

A column of black smoke rose into the sky on the southern horizon.

Her heart pounding, Cricket turned to Sundew. "What is that?" she asked. "Did the LeafWings do that?"

"I don't know," Sundew said, and for once her frown looked worried instead of angry. "They didn't tell me they — I mean, they weren't supposed to —"

Cricket threw open her wings and flew to the top of the cliff, high above the sea. From here, on a clear day, you could almost see to the far ends of the continent.

This was not a clear day, but she could still see the spire of Wasp Hive to the west and Jewel Hive in the southwest. The column of smoke came from beyond Jewel Hive, farther south.

"It's not Jewel Hive," Sundew said, landing beside her.

"Bloodworm Hive," Cricket said.

"Yes." The LeafWing stared out at the smoke as though it was something she'd ordered at a café, but it had come in the wrong color and covered with maggots. "They went ahead and did it. Without waiting for me." She blew out a long exhale.

"All those dragonets," Cricket said, feeling as if her roots had been sliced off. "The eggs in their Nest. The SilkWings who can't fly." She closed her eyes. *Could I have saved them? If I'd been faster and smarter and found the answers sooner?*

"They *said* they would wait for my report. But I guess they were LYING ABOUT THAT." Sundew looked sincerely angry, in a different way than usual, Cricket thought. "Maybe they didn't care what I was doing. Maybe they were just planting their seeds for the last six days, moving all the pieces into place."

"Did you know all the pieces?" Cricket asked numbly. "Did you know what they were planning?"

Sundew hesitated. "I knew most of it. This plan was in motion before we met you. But I thought — I really thought they'd wait for me." She ducked her head to look sideways at Cricket. "One thing changed, though. Because of you three, we learned about the Chrysalis. I wouldn't have believed they existed, before . . . I mean, that SilkWings could even think about fighting back. We found Bloodworm Hive's Chrysalis and gave them a message to evacuate their dragonets from the Hive and to stay out of the webs last night."

Cricket shot her a look. "I'm sure that didn't arouse suspicion at all."

"You'd be surprised how little attention your tribe pays to what SilkWings do," Sundew said pointedly.

They were silent for another moment.

"I'm sure they'll get the eggs out, too," Sundew offered, shifting uncomfortably on her talons. "Once they realize they can't save the Hive, that's the first thing the HiveWings will do."

"I hope you're right," Cricket said. "I hope someone remembers the SilkWings in their cocoons, too."

Something swooped across the sky to her right and Sundew tugged her down, throwing her wing over Cricket's back so they were both flat to the earth and partly camouflaged by Sundew's green scales.

HiveWings were swarming toward Bloodworm Hive, hundreds of them rising from Wasp Hive and Jewel Hive and somewhere farther north; Yellowjacket Hive, Cricket guessed. They flew like a cloud of bats across the sky, south to the burning city. Queen Wasp was sending her Hive mind to try to save it.

Cricket clutched Sundew's arm. "Right now," she said.

"Right now what?"

"Now is the time to burn her greenhouse." Cricket pointed at the dragons disappearing into the distance. "Everyone's flying to Bloodworm Hive. It's the perfect distraction."

"It's not a distraction," Sundew objected. "It's a blow for justice!"

"Well, we can *use it* as a distraction," Cricket said. "To do something that might actually help dragons instead of hurting anyone. If we go *right now.*"

"My parents," Sundew said, glancing at the smoke again. "I'm supposed to wait for them — I'm not authorized for another mission."

"Seriously?" Cricket arched her eyebrows at the LeafWing. "You need to wait for *permission*? You?"

"No," Sundew barked. "I'm just wondering where they are, that's all! I don't need them! Let's go kill some plants!

Oof, no, I don't like the sound of that at all. Let's go destroy some HiveWing stuff! That's much better."

Bumblebee did not wake up as Cricket wrapped her in her scarf sling and tucked her into her chest. She snorted and gruffled and stuck sharp little claws into her, but Cricket poked the fish back into her mouth and Bumblebee dozed off again.

They flew along the south coast of the peninsula, staying below the level of the cliffs to avoid being spotted. Cricket noticed that Swordtail couldn't keep his eyes off the bay; he kept turning to search the beach below them. The fifth time he crashed into Sundew by accident, she nearly threw him into the ocean.

She glanced at Blue and saw him turning to look out at the islands, too.

Oh, she realized. *They're looking for Luna.*

I hope she's all right. I hope her flamesilk is helping to keep her safe.

There were no more HiveWings in the sky when they reached the grassland on the outskirts of Wasp Hive. They landed and slipped into the shadow of one of the greenhouses. Cricket could still see the smoke in the distance, now with small figures wheeling around it.

"If Bloodworm Hive falls," Blue said, leaning against her side, "so do the webs between it and Mantis Hive and Jewel Hive. That's a lot of SilkWing homes."

Sundew hunched her shoulders and dug her claws into the ground. "I'll go scout ahead." She hurried off between the glass walls.

"It's weird," Blue said, watching her go. "The posters always said the LeafWings were going to do something terrible to the Hives, and I always believed it until we met Sundew. And then, the more I knew her, I guess I started thinking the LeafWings would all be like her . . . mad on the outside but kind on the inside, right? Like, of course she *could* blow up a whole Hive and maybe she'd even want to, but she wouldn't actually do it. So I thought none of them would actually do it. But now they have. So was Queen Wasp right and I was wrong? I don't know what to think."

"I think you're still right," Cricket said. "I mean, that Sundew wouldn't have done it herself. And I hope there are other LeafWings like her." She looked south again, at the smoke that seemed to be painted onto the clouds forever now. Did this mean the HiveWings and LeafWings were at war again? It felt so clear to her that they shouldn't be. They all had one enemy, the same enemy: Queen Wasp. If only she could get them to see that.

But she was just one little dragon. How could she get anyone to listen to her?

Sundew appeared around a corner of a greenhouse and

beckoned to them. They hurried to her on silent talons through the wet grass.

"Just two guards patrolling the greenhouses, as far as I can see," she said in a low voice. "Hard to tell from a distance, but they seem to have their own eyes. If we keep quiet, I think we can sneak past them."

"FLORBLE!" announced Bumblebee, popping her head out of the sling around Cricket.

Sundew gave her a steely look. "Don't even think about it, dragonet."

"BLEEMORK!" Bumblebee retorted at top volume. She squirmed around in the sling, pulled out the fish, which had not improved in smell over the course of the morning, and flung it at Sundew's head.

"I *beg* your pardon," Sundew said, catching the fish and waving it at Bumblebee. "This was a perfectly good breakfast and it's your own fault you're hungry if you don't want to eat it."

"SMEEBO SMEEBO SMEEBO!" Bumblebee said in the same tone, wagging her claw at Sundew.

"Listen here," Sundew said with a scowl. "We are on a STEALTH HORTICULTURAL MISSION and you are going to be ABSOLUTELY SILENT until we are done, do you understand?"

"Loobleflooblegooble," Bumblebee burbled, reaching toward Sundew with her front talons. "Herkleturklemisshoo."

"Nope. No. No, sir. Cricket, control your tiny monster."

"I think she wants you," Cricket admitted. The dragonet was vigorously wiggling her way out of the sling, no matter how Cricket tried to pin her down.

"Well, too bad!" Sundew snapped.

"BOO BAH!" Bumblebee shouted enthusiastically.

"Shhhhhh!" Swordtail tried, flapping his wings at her.

Cricket hadn't realized a dragonet that small could laugh already. Bumblebee's whole face wrinkled up and she fell back into the sling, giggling hysterically.

"So," Sundew said to Cricket. "This is officially the worst idea you've ever had."

"She might be quieter if you take her," Cricket suggested.

"I'm not sure," Blue said. "I think she likes it when you yell at her."

"Here," Sundew said, digging into one of her pouches. "Give her this."

"I'm not sticking a sleepflower up a baby dragonet's nose," Cricket said protectively. "Or a centipede or a paralysis dart or whatever else you have in there."

"It's just dried mango," Sundew said. "Even I have yet to use a paralysis toxin on a baby dragonet." She scowled at Bumblebee. "The key word there is YET, howler monkey."

"Yim yim yim," Bumblebee agreed cheerfully, snatching the mango out of Sundew's talons and stuffing it in her mouth. Her eyes went wide and she gave Sundew a worshipful look. "YIMMMM."

"What is this feeling of doom that just settled on me?" Sundew asked the sky.

"You *did* have mango!" Swordtail said to her accusingly.

"Can we please get on with bringing down the HiveWing queen now?" Sundew said to Bumblebee. The dragonet ignored her, snuggled into Cricket, and went to work on the mango.

Swordtail and Sundew went first, padding swiftly through the aisles. Cricket felt a weird shiver of déjà vu, remembering the last time they were sneaking through these same greenhouses, early in the morning. That was before the queen knew Cricket's secret, when Cricket still had the option of going home.

That was before I knew her secrets, too.

But now I do. I have the truth in my talons and I'm going to do something with it.

The queen's greenhouse loomed up before them, crowded with dark green leaves that pressed against the glass windows. Cricket couldn't believe they'd been here before, standing in the middle of the queen's secret, and hadn't even realized it.

One guard stood outside the door, idly reading the warning sign. His tail flicked back and forth across the grass, leaving a silvery trail through the wet blades. He didn't look very worried about anyone coming to do battle with the plants.

Sundew reached into one of her pouches and softly drew out a tiny hollow tube. She slipped something sharp into one end, raised the other to her mouth, and blew the dart at the guard.

His tail went still on the grass; his wings stopped midflutter. His whole body was frozen in place.

"FLORB," Bumblebee said approvingly around the mango.

"Drag him away from the greenhouse," Sundew said to Swordtail. "He doesn't need to go up in flames with it."

Cricket and Blue exchanged glances. *She's saving a random HiveWing. She's making sure he doesn't die.* Cricket didn't think Sundew would have done that before she knew them. *If we could change her mind, maybe we can change others.*

Swordtail grappled with the paralyzed dragon while the other three sliced away the webs covering the greenhouse door and stepped inside. The heat and humidity swamped Cricket just as it had before. And now she recognized the smell, too, sharp and unpleasant amid the other scents of the plants around them.

"It's this one," Sundew said, lifting a leaf on one of the vines that thronged the greenhouse, circling and choking the other plants. The stem of the vine was dark red with veins of bright green, and the leaves were the same in reverse, bright green with veins of red like streams of blood. Each was the size of a dragon talon with jagged, tough edges. It would have been perfectly appropriately creepy if it weren't for the clusters of tiny white flowers nestled between the leaves.

Sundew rubbed the leaf between her claws for a moment, frowning at it. "I don't know what it is," she said at length.

"Me neither," Cricket offered. "I don't remember seeing it in any of my botany books, and I think I would."

"I know someone who might know." Sundew used her claws to slice through the vine in two spots, making a cutting as long as her arm. She rolled it into a loose ball and tucked it into an empty pouch.

"Is that a good idea?" Blue asked. "Shouldn't we destroy all of it, so it can never grow again and no one can ever use it like she has?"

"I think we need to know what it is," Sundew said to him.

"Me too," Cricket agreed. "And maybe . . ." She hesitated, afraid to say it out loud.

"Maybe there's an antidote," Sundew finished for her.

Blue's eyes widened.

"Smorg bamfibo," Bumblebee declared in Sundew's solemnest voice.

"I feel like you're mocking me," Sundew said to the dragonet.

"Smeeg smog smockeefee," the dragonet answered with enormous gravity, copying Sundew's frown.

Sundew raised one eyebrow at Cricket.

"I swear I did not teach her to do that," Cricket promised.

"All right," Sundew said, turning to sweep the greenhouse with her gaze. "Who wants to burn it all down?"

There was a pause before she turned and leveled her gaze on Blue.

"Oh, right, me," Blue said. He stepped to the nearest cluster of vines and set his front talons on them. Fiery silk erupted from his wrists, catching and tangling through the leaves. Everywhere it touched, blades of flame flickered, smoked, curled into black ash or brightened into orange blossoms of fire.

Heavy reddish-green smoke rose from the vines and Cricket covered her snout with one of her scarves. "Don't breathe it in!" she shouted at the others. She wrapped another scarf around Bumblebee's indignant face. "Blue, let's go!" She tugged on his arm and turned to run to the door with Sundew.

Blue followed them, pausing every few steps to shoot more fountains of flame over the vines. Cricket could hear the crackling fire building and spreading. The heat shot past tolerable and pressed against her scales, and she thought of the dragons in Bloodworm Hive, and wondered if this was what they'd felt as they fled their burning city.

They threw open the door and tumbled onto the wet grass outside. Blue leaped out after them and slammed the door behind him, but it splintered into a million pieces as it hit the frame. Glass fragments exploded outward along with tongues of fire, roaring like angry dragons.

Cricket curled her body around Bumblebee and ran to escape the flames and smoke. She nearly collided head-on with the second HiveWing guard, who started to grab her and then froze, staring openmouthed at the burning greenhouse.

"That one is lost," Cricket said, shaking her. "Get water and you can save the others. Make sure your friend is safe, too." She turned to look around and saw the paralyzed guard lying a few greenhouses away; Swordtail was still trying to drag him a little farther. The grass was wet enough that Cricket hoped the fire wouldn't spread, but she wasn't sure. She didn't want the other greenhouses to burn. They held the food and other resources for hundreds of dragons. Sundew's parents might have been willing to burn them, but she thought Sundew wouldn't.

The guard pointed at the greenhouse. "The queen," she stammered. "She — that's her —"

Cricket gripped her shoulders to get her attention. "That is where she kept the plant that lets her control us," she said. "I saw her stabbing eggs in the Jewel Hive nest. She injects us before we've even hatched, do you understand? That plant gave her the Hive-mind power, and we burned it to take it away from her."

"What?" The guard shook her head, confused. "No, the queen — she has that power because she's our queen —"

"She had it because of a plant," Cricket said. "She's been poisoning us, our whole tribe, ever since the Tree Wars, maybe longer. You have to tell everyone."

The guard looked terrified. "Me?"

"Yes," Cricket said. "Knowing the truth isn't enough if you don't share it. Everyone needs to know."

"I . . . I have to save the greenhouses," the guard said, pulling out of Cricket's grip. She turned and ran toward the Hive.

"She'll be back with help soon," Blue said at Cricket's shoulder.

"Swordtail, are you napping?" Sundew shouted. "Let's GO!"

Swordtail leaped away from the guard and into the sky. The others spread their wings and joined him, and Cricket swerved around a plume of smoke as it erupted from the greenhouse roof.

They soared away, toward a looming bank of dark clouds in the north. Cricket beat her wings as hard as she could and glanced down at Bumblebee, who had somehow managed to fall asleep again despite all the commotion.

They flew and flew, following Sundew, until Wasp Hive was far behind them. There was no sign of any pursuers. Cricket hoped that all of Queen Wasp's attention was on Bloodworm Hive, and that she wouldn't even discover the fire in her greenhouse until she returned home.

Home — there's a thing I don't have anymore.

"Sundew!" she called. "Where are we going? Shouldn't we go back to the cave to find your parents?"

Sundew glanced over her shoulder, her green and gold scales somehow still shining even in the grayest sky. "I'm not waiting around for them," she called back. "They'll expect to meet me back home."

"Where's that?" Cricket asked, catching up to her. "Are we going to where the other LeafWings are?" Her pulse sped up despite her worries and her sadness over Bloodworm Hive. At last, she was going to find out how the LeafWings had survived the Tree Wars and where they'd been hiding all this time.

"Has anyone ever told you that you ask a lot of questions?" Sundew said wryly.

"All the time," Cricket said, smiling back.

"Well, I'm surprised you haven't guessed this answer by now." Sundew pointed her snout north, closing her eyes as a gust of wind and rain rippled over their scales.

"That way?" Cricket said. "You mean — all the way that way? Are you saying the LeafWings are in . . ." She trailed off, remembering the stories she'd read about carnivorous plants ten times the size of a dragon, of toxins and snakes and quicksand and deadly vines and venomous wasps and all the many, many ways a dragon could die up there.

"Yes," said Sundew, smiling a real smile now. "We're going home to the Poison Jungle."

EPILOGUE

"I'm not sure this was a good idea," Tsunami said to Turtle. She wasn't sure why she was whispering; they appeared to be alone in the jungle, and yet it also felt as if there were hundreds of eyes watching their every move.

The tangled trees seemed to be reaching for them with long trailing roots, and branches like skeletal fingers slid into the water. The sand under them had become oozing mud and she couldn't see anything through the silt and foggy green haze in the river.

At least, she'd thought it was a river . . . a river they could follow into the interior of the continent. But as the banks closed in and the jutting rocks got sharper, she was getting the distinct sensation of swimming into a very large, shark-like mouth.

She paused, treading water for a moment and turning in a circle. Something enormously long and scaly broke the surface of the river for a moment, and Tsunami readied her claws — but the snake only lifted its head to study them with cold eyes, then rippled away.

Turtle, luckily, had not seen it. He had found a boulder to clutch, panting. She kept forgetting to set her pace slower for him, although she'd been doing it for days.

Somewhere in the middle of the vast ocean, they'd both had a small panic attack, wondering if there was really anything out there, or whether they'd missed it, or whether they were going in the wrong direction and would end up swimming for a thousand years without ever seeing land again. That was when Tsunami had realized why SeaWings had never made this journey before. They might be creatures of the sea, but they needed land, too. They would not swim for days with no end in sight, with no certainty that they would ever find anything.

"Let's go back," Tsunami said to her brother. "Let's find another place to land, more like what Luna described."

"Yeah," he gasped. "I thought she said there weren't any trees."

"Maybe she meant 'only terrifying trees,'" Tsunami said, looking up at the vines oozing off the branches overhead.

"Don't. Move."

The voice that suddenly spoke from the bank had an odd accent and a note of authority that made Tsunami freeze obediently before her ears had even caught up to the instructions.

"Um," Turtle started.

"Don't speak, either," said the voice. "One . . . two . . ."

A dark green shape hurtled past Tsunami's head and smashed into the snake as it lunged out of the water at them. All Tsunami could see for a moment was a blur of claws and fangs and scales thrashing; she had to close her eyes against the waves kicked violently into her face.

Finally the river went still, and she dared to open her eyes again.

A green dragon with brown eyes hovered overhead, clutching the dead snake in her talons. Her wings were paler green than her body and shaped like leaves, and her under-scales were dappled with dark green leaf shapes like shadows.

"Three moons," Turtle said. "Thank you."

"Really, really, really thank you," Tsunami echoed, almost too bewildered to speak.

"What kind of dragons are you?" the stranger asked, flinging the snake back into the river.

"We're SeaWings," Tsunami answered, trying to recover her equilibrium. "I'm Tsunami, and this is Turtle. We're from the other side of the ocean."

"I'm Willow," said the green dragon, "and if you want to live, you should turn around and go back there right now."

Moon found Luna sitting on the farthest edge of the beach again, staring out toward Pantala with the ocean whispering over her claws. Luna twisted toward the little black dragon as she approached and was startled by the grim look on Moon's face. She'd started to think Moon only ever looked either perfectly serene or mildly concerned.

"What is it?" Luna asked. "A vision?"

"Yes," Moon said, her gaze shifting toward the horizon. "A vision. Cities burning, dragons hurting one another, more dragons being terrible just because other dragons are different from them, just like all my visions." She stopped for a moment and rubbed her forehead.

"Does that mean we're going there? You've thought of a way to get to Pantala?"

Moon shook her head. "No." She looked out at Luna's distant home again, and Luna imagined she could almost see the flames and screaming dragons reflected in Moon's dark green eyes.

"We don't need to," Moon said. "They're coming to us."

WINGS OF FIRE

will continue . . .

DISCOVER THE #1 *NEW YORK TIMES* BESTSELLING SERIES!

THE DRAGONET PROPHECY

THE JADE MOUNTAIN PROPHECY

THE LOST CONTINENT PROPHECY

LEGENDS

GRAPHIC NOVELS

EBOOK SHORT STORIES

SCHOLASTIC

scholastic.com/WingsOfFire

WOF13